My Spicy Red Hot Holiday Collection

Just Bae

Contents

Ebenezer

Liam

Tanya

Ebenezer

Chapter One

"Marley was dead, to begin with."

Tina rolled her eyes.

"And I loath Christmas," I added, ignoring her deepening scowl.

"Ebb, I need you. Moral support. Please." Her features softened, plaintively trying to appeal to my more generous side - despite knowing I didn't have one.

I merely shook my head and returned to the layout on the screen.

"Just so you can bonk Carrie or Caris," she muttered under her breath.

I didn't bother looking up as she sighed and moved away, though I'll admit I almost felt a flicker of guilt for leaving her to the wolves she called family. Damn Christmas spirit must be infectious if I was feeling guilty. I quickly dismissed that idea.

Technically I am an orphan - an adult one, but still an orphan, so I don't have to worry about family responsibilities over the festive season. My parents had me late in life, both on their third marriage, and a baby was not part of their plans. When they found out they were pregnant at Christmas, their shock resulted in the cruel joke: they had named me Ebenezer. Unintentionally my parents' humour had left me with a dislike of Christmas. The taunting and bullying by boys at boarding school was bad enough, but adults had never hesitated to crack Scrooge-related jokes either.

Mum and Dad loved me, but in reality, a variety of distant relatives brought me up so my parents could pursue more adult activities. One lasting memory of my father was him repeatedly telling me, "Ebbie, only ever do what makes you happy." That had become my life's mantra: if I didn't enjoy it, I didn't do it.

Dad died the year I graduated; Mum was only 18 months behind him. The inheritance allowed me to move to London and pursue a career in journalism. It funded a two-year internship with a leading national rag. My parents' deaths had meant, ultimately, I was now a commercial editor and taking home a healthy salary. The money and lifestyle did make me happy. Cheers, Dad.

Tina started at the paper after me, and over the last ten years, I guess you could say we had become best friends. Whatever that title meant. No matter how outlandish my extracurricular escapades, she was the person I'd sit in Costa with and laugh with the next day. Our mutual dark sense of humour put us on the same wavelength.

I'd first met her eccentric Uncle Marley at her thirtieth birthday party seven years ago. Hedonistic was the only word to describe him. He spent the night regaling me with stories about booze-filled debauchery, exotic extended holidays and scantily clothed girls less than half his age. He'd burned his way through his money, as he always said, "You can't take it with you."That man had been instantly elevated to my perfect role model.

I had willingly attended as Tina's plus-one the next Christmas just to see my new hero. It was the best Christmas I could remember. I spent the day drinking whiskey, smoking and bantering with Marley. Tina's family frowned upon the black sheep of the family, but I guess a sense of responsibility for their eternal-bachelor uncle meant they invited him around every year. Tina's mother was so overjoyed the detrimental impact of her filthy brother was being kept contained and away from the grandchildren, she insisted I attend every Christmas since.

But Marley was dead. There was no doubt whatever about that. Tina remained tight-lipped regarding the precise circumstances. The fact attractive, twenty-something-year-old twins had announced his demise on

Twitter straight after calling the paramedics, and the coroner recording a heart attack as the cause of death told me most of the details. In death, Marley was still the epitome of the man I wanted to be.

Without his charismatic presence, I would not subject myself to Tina's overly jovial, festive family. Sure, I diluted the questions and knowing glares of her parents and brother as they quizzed her why she wasn't married and churning out rugrats yet. My arm casually slung over her shoulder, the odd peck on the cheek and flowers for her mother gave me the status of doting 'fake' boyfriend.

I don't know how Tina explained away the lack of engagement ring or baby bump. I didn't care either - work focused, infertility, whatever she had needed to pacify them was no skin off my nose, but this year helping her out didn't win against my alternative arrangements.

For the last seven years, I had turfed the latest conquest out of my bed on Christmas morning, then done the long drive up to Shropshire to play Tina's partner. But with no Marley, it meant I had no lure. Instead, fucking Kerry through the 25th seemed a good way to honour his memory.

"I'll ditch our Boxing Day tradition, if you'll just give me Christmas Day." Tina's voice dragged me from my reverie.

I looked at her blankly.

Her hands rested on her hips, demanding my attention. Suddenly the defiance of negotiation faded and her shoulders slumped as she looked crestfallen.

"Huh?" I furrowed my forehead trying to catch up.

"Don't worry about it. Have a good Christmas." With a dismissive wave of her hand, she walked away again.

I closed my eyes slowly and sighed. Damn. Since I had been spending Christmas with her family, we had driven home through the night and she crashed at mine. The next day was spent lounging in my apartment, eating leftovers her mum sent us back with and watching Die Hard - the best Christmas movie ever. I wouldn't have described it as a 'tradition' but she was right, we had slipped into the routine.

I honestly didn't think she would still be planning our mutual Boxing Day veg-out; she knew I had Kerry staying until the 27th. What did she expect? I hadn't even thought about seeing Tina this year. Now I felt like a royal arse, she was a friend and a good one at that. I picked up my phone and tapped out a quick message.

"Day after Boxing Day, mine, 11.00. I've got salmon and Buck's Fizz. I'll even let you watch Home Alone after our Bruce Willis fix."

Feeling much better I'd done my good deed for the day I returned to finishing the copy I was working on.

* * *

Kerry had the most perfect breasts. I've always been a fun-bags man but hers took that pleasure to a whole new level. Sure, they were surgically enhanced, but those expensive silicone implants meant sliding my cock between them was pure and unadulterated bliss.

She peered through heavy lids, the false lashes framing dark, lust-filled eyes.

"Merry Christmas, Ebb." Her drool-covered face glistened in the low light of my bedroom.

I groaned, remembering that luscious, pouty mouth enclosed around my cock. That girl knew what to do with her tongue, and her stamina was epic. Before my cock had made its way between those welcoming breasts she'd worshipped me for a good half an hour.

The illuminated clock radio showed it was nearly midnight. Kerry shifted her hands and pressed the breasts tighter around me. I worked my jaw, it felt so good. Her drool acted as a perfect lubricated slick. She smiled and poked out that magical tongue so it flicked over my slit each time the head emerged from its warm breast cavern. I rocked my hips faster feeling the orgasm approaching.

A minute to midnight, Big Ben would be chiming in Christmas any second. What a great start to the day to cover Kerry's flawless face with my cum. My balls tightened and abdominals tensed. Ecstasy only moments away.

"Merry Christmas," I growled.

The first rope shot across her nose. She shut her eyes as the second landed higher. Her mouth opened, searching for my cum. Marley would have been proud.

It felt so good, I couldn't breathe. I tried to drag air into my lungs, but nothing happened. My cock exploded again - painfully this time. Jerking and spasming, I lost control of my body and fell backwards.

Face up, flat on the bed between Kerry's legs I couldn't move. My cock was on fire. More agonising cum shot straight into the air and my vision blurred.

Pain ricocheted through my body.

My balls were being crushed. No dominatrix heels could match the agony. Gasping, like a fish out of water, my life flashed before me.

Death was coming, but the sensation of my cock and balls being ripped from my body meant I welcomed it with open arms. Anything to relieve this sadistic torture.

My cock still erupted and now it felt like a burning razor wire was exploding from my guts.

I blacked out.

Coming to, bathed in a cold sweat, the first thing I registered was the pain was gone. Numb, that's all I felt, numb. I sucked in a noisy breath and cautiously opened my eyes. I was still flat on the bed but bright light filled the room. I might be numb but I wasn't dead, thank fuck for that. Kerry had gone, she must have gotten up to call for help.

My hand quickly checked to reassure me my cock and balls were still firmly attached. Carefully I sat up... and screamed!

Scrabbling backwards towards the headboard I tried to escape.

Before me stood Marley, or some apparition of him. His flesh was translucent and not a shred of clothing covered his aged, wrinkled frame. He had the same wicked smile but his beady eyes stared lifelessly at me.

Not daring to look away, I slid my hand along the headboard to pull myself towards the door.

"Sit still, boy," Marley said with icy breath.

Heart pounding, I froze and shook as my eyes scanned the thing before me.

Its... his body was weighed down by a thick jute rope. Hanging from the rope, like tree decorations, were assorted dildos and jewelled butt plugs of every size, colour and style. Some were quietly buzzing as the Marley-thing moved a step closer. He walked wide-legged due to the large silver cock cage encasing his manhood; a heavy padlock held the contraption tight shut. Shiny steel cuffs wrapped around each ankle and clattered on the floor with every laboured step.

I opened my mouth to scream again, but before I

could make a noise Marley emitted a blood-curdling wail. The window rattled and I threw my hands over my ears. It felt like a thousand rods of fire were penetrating my skull. The sound ripped my soul out.

I was dead and Marley my escort to hell.

His mouth shut and the death call ceased.

"What do you want with me?" I managed when my faculties returned.

"Much," the apparition replied, billows of frosted air plumed from its nose.

"Who are you?" I said through chattering teeth.

"Ask me who I was," it corrected.

"Okay, who were you?" I furrowed my brow, already knowing the answer and not liking it.

"In life, I was Marley Jacobs." The clouds of breath continued with each deliberately spoken word.

"Er... can you sit down?" I waved a hand towards the bucket chair in the far corner of my room.

"I can."

"Then do it." I tried to put confidence into my wavering voice. If he did as I asked it'd at least move him away from me.

The ghost took the seat, his lifeless eyes still locked on me.

"You don't believe me," he said, pulling the rope so the menagerie of sex toys piled up in his lap.

"No, I don't." I pressed my back against the headboard

wanting all the distance I could get from the monstrosity before me.

"Why do you doubt your senses?"

"Because..." I paused to consider my answer. "Drink... I've just cum... er... it must be a thing. Overloaded my senses-"

Marley shook a large black dildo at me and that appalling noise flooded from him again.

I clawed my nails into the headboard wishing he'd stop before my room imploded on itself. Suddenly he threw the dildo at me. It hit me as I scrambled away and fell off the bed and onto my knees.

Not knowing what else to do I clasped my hands over my face. "Have mercy! Why me?"

"Do you believe it is me now?"

"Yes. Yes. I do." I parted my fingers to look at the poltergeist. "Spirits walk the earth, but why come to me?"

"It is required of all men for their spirit to walk among fellowmen. If they fail to do that in life they are condemned to walk far and wide in death. They are doomed to travel the earth for eternity, so they might witness what they never experienced in life - happiness."

Despite being chilled to the core of my bone marrow his words didn't make sense. I dropped my hands away to peer up at his black holes of eyes.

"You went everywhere." I tilted my head in confusion. "And with many people. You were happy."

Marley angrily grabbed the rope and yanked, making the attached erotica bounce and clatter.

"What's with the mobile Ann Summers store?" I didn't feel humorous but it seemed like the only defence I had left.

"I wear the bondage I created in life. Every vibrator, cuff and dildo crafted by my own hands. I spent my whole life in the eternal search for ecstasy." Marley leaned forward letting some of the toy-filled rope fall to his feet like a grotesque sexualised snake. "Does this not sound familiar to you?"

I shook harder.

“You will know," Marley continued. "You wear your own bondage."

My eyes fell to the floor, expecting to see toys, leather and rope surrounded me, but there was nothing.

I looked up at Marley. "C'mon, help me out."

"I can't, I have no help to give," he replied. "Help comes from other places. From kind good people. I can not help myself, I can not stop or linger. I must serve my time, sentenced to move forever."

A shard of relief registered upon hearing he couldn't linger. The sooner Marley was gone the better. My hand rubbed my chin. I could always think clearer when touching my face.

"So go back to walking the earth," I said with far more defiance than I knew I had.

Marley looked wistful - as much as a ghost with lifeless eyes can. "I wasted my life. I am doomed to hard labour while the people who lived enjoy the afterlife."

"You lived life to the full," I countered quickly.

"Sex!" Marley wailed. "It was fucking and nothing more. Humanity and love fill the air at Christmas so I am forced to be surrounded by the souls of others, to inhale their happiness as penance of what I never had."

An icy shiver travelled down my spine.

"My time is nearly up."

Thank fuck for that.

"Listen to me."

"I'm listening." I sat a little straighter, still on my knees.

"I don't know how you can see me now. I have been beside you many days since I died."

I shuddered and nervously wiped sweat from my forehead. The idea of that thing following me around was not pleasant.

"I'm here to warn you and tell you you still have a chance of hope. A chance to save yourself, Ebenezer."

"You were always a good friend. Thank you." I couldn't quite believe I was thanking him, but my response was automatic.

"You will be haunted," Marley continued. "Three ghosts."

I swallowed hard, this didn't sound like a great

outcome. One Marley-ghost was more than enough for a lifetime.

"I'd rather not," I muttered.

"Without them, you have no hope of finding happiness and saving yourself from the fate I suffer. The first will come at the stroke of one."

"Could they all come together? Get it over and done with," I suggested hopefully.

Marley ignored me. "The second will come when the clock chimes two. At three the last ghost will visit you. Remember what I have told you."

I watched with my mouth open unable to find any words as he stood and walked backwards, dragging the erotic bondage. With each slow, laboured step the window behind him slowly opened. He paused and beckoned me.

I got to my feet shakily and followed his retreating form. Abruptly he held up a hand. Fear and surprise rooted me to the spot.

Outside I could hear a pitiful chaos of wailing. Marley softly joined in the crescendo of noise.

Curiosity got the better of me and I lean forward to peer through the open window. The air was filled with phantoms aimlessly wandering through the bleak, dark night. The misery was thick as Marley passed through the window and joined the lost souls.

A fog swirled from the street below, lifting and

shrouding the ghosts until all I could see was a thick London pea soup.

I quickly closed the window, locking it shut, and turned to examine my room. It looked the same as I had always remembered it. Picking up my phone I checked the time. Half-past midnight, Christmas morning.

What the fuck just happened?

I sat on the edge of the bed and put my head in my hands.

Stave 2: The First of the Three Spirits

"Back in the land of the living?" Kerry laughed, her hands massaging my thighs.

I groaned and peeled my eyelids open. It took a moment to reorient. Her glorious naked body crouched over me, hard nipples grazing my skin as her fingers worked their way higher. My cock twitched at the sight and sensation. Still playing mental catch-up on what had just happened, I glanced at the clock. The digits told me it was five past midnight.

What?That made no sense. I mentally ran through the last half hour... but there was no half hour. How could only five minutes have passed?

Kerry blew warm, wet breath over my cock.

"Hmmm," I mumbled. Damn, that was a cool trick.

I dragged my focus back to the exquisite creature

ministering to my body and wound my fingers into her auburn locks. Her tongue teased my balls then slid along my shaft. With a dip of her chin, she took my cock into her eager mouth.

"Yes, baby." My head fell back on the pillow. I'd hit the jackpot meeting this girl.

A vision of Marley flickered across my memory. I swallowed uncomfortably and looked down at Kerry resting on my thighs. I needed to concentrate on her and her alone.

She peered up, cheeks hollowed as slurps filled the room. Sucking and licking in the perfect balance of bliss.

A nightmare. That's what it must have been. I pushed away all thoughts of Marley.

My cock grew and filled with each expert lap of her tongue. Precum oozed and the familiar feeling of ecstasy built. My mind finally blank, I relaxed.

She was incredible, just holding me on the edge of orgasm. Massaging and teasing, even humming against me. Fuck, it felt good.

They say time flies when you're having fun, but I was still surprised to see the clock announcing it was almost one am. A swirl of Kerry's malleable tongue made my balls tighten.

"Baby, I'm gonna cum."

Her hand wrapped around me, expertly sliding and turning. She lifted her mouth and drool webbed from my cock to her chin. Right then I knew I'd never seen anything so beautiful.

"Merry Christmas, Ebb." Her hand tightened and pumped.

She angled me towards her open mouth.

"Baby!" I yelled as my orgasm hit.

Big Ben chimed.

Fuuuuuck, noooo!

The pain was back.

Hand too tight. Wrenching. Twisting. Yanking.

Fuck!

"Stop!"

She gripped harder.

Teeth embedded in my sensitive flesh.

Nooooo-

I passed out.

Chapter Two

Even though my closed eyelids, I could see light. Wincing, I cracked an eye open. Tears flooded my vision in response to the brightness. I blinked rapidly to clear the mist.

I wished I hadn't.

Before me stood the most peculiar creature.

I rolled onto my side to stare at the thing beside the bed. It was the height of a child, with the body of an old woman. Breasts sagging low, pubes sparse and grey, loose skin hung off withered thighs and wasted arms.

I scanned up, closed my eyes and opened them again to confirm what I could see. She was beautiful with a flawless, almost angelic face. There was a glow emanating like a halo around her long golden hair.

If I could just hide her body, the hideous onslaught on my eyes below her neck would be gone. Thinking surprisingly clearly - considering this must be another nightmare - I scooted across the bed and grabbed my dressing gown.

"Here." I offered it to the woman.

Gnarled aged fingers grazed mine as she took it. I was surprised at the softness and warmth of her touch. I sat on the edge of the bed as she wrapped my far-too-large dressing gown around her grotesque body. I rubbed my chin and considered my next move while I waited for her childlike innocent eyes to look at me.

"Are you the ghost Marley mentioned?" I asked casually, much easier to do now I could only see her beautiful face.

"I am." She smiled warmly, her voice had a soft song-like quality.

"Who, or what are you?" The calmness was infectious as I relaxed in her presence.

"I am the Ghost of Christmas Past," she told me melodically.

"Long past?" I asked hopefully.

She lost her welcoming smile and scowled. "No, your past."

Damn. Why couldn't I have dreamed Disney's Mickey's Christmas Carol version? A few cartoon spirits would be far easier to deal with than this horror show.

"Why are you here?"

"Your welfare." Her smile returned but it was menacing and false.

"My welfare would be a whole lot better if you could just go."

Apparently, this was the wrong thing to say. I jumped when she reached out and grasped my arm. It was both a light sensual touch while also being firm enough I knew I could not break free.

"Come with me," she said, pulling my arm.

With no choice, I stood up and towered over her dwarf body, but the grip on my arm didn't slacken. She tugged me towards the window. I gulped, this might just be a dream but jumping out of the eighth storey was not going to end well for me. I tried to resist.

"I can't... I'll die," I stuttered when my efforts to stop were futile.

She paused and peered up. I looked at her beauty, and an unexplainable peace washed over me. So enamoured by the sight I hardly noticed as she lay a hand on my chest.

"You may now travel with me." Without hesitating, she stepped through the window.

Surprising myself I went with her willingly. She made me feel anything was possible. Her touch gave me hope.

Outside the window, the city had vanished. The dark, foggy night had been replaced by a cold, clear winter's day. I was standing on the grass in front of my parents' home... my home.

"What the..." I trailed off in disbelief. Before me was my father and... me, or at least my seventeen-year-old self.

"You remember?" the ghost said.

"Of course." My eyes misted.

Mariah Carey's 'All I Want for Christmas is You' blared from a speaker positioned by an open window. Dad was on a ladder and I stood below him, passing up a colourful string of lights. We were both singing but my hormonally breaking voice mutilated the tune, causing us both to laugh.

I felt a tear track down my face.

"What is the matter?" the ghost asked.

"Nothing." I quickly wiped my eyes.

"Strange you have forgotten the love."

I gave a strangled sob, unsure why the people before me could not hear my pitiful cry. The ghost must have read my mind, her small hand found mine and our fingers intertwined. The touch was reassuring.

My mother came out of the house, carrying a plate of hot mince pies. Dad noticed her first, he gave a joyous yell and slid down the ladder. In two strides he was beside her. He wrapped her waist in his arms and moved behind, making Mum giggle as he kissed her neck.

I laughed seeing my younger face light up.

"Ebby, find yourself a good woman and you'll be happy for life," Dad said, hooking his chin over her shoulder and looking at my younger self. "Only do what makes you happy."

Loneliness washed over me; the ghost was right, I had forgotten the love of my family. I'd forgotten how much my parents loved me. I bit my lower lip to stop it trembling. If the guys in the office had seen me they would not have believed it as I alternated between laughing and crying watching the happy family.

"What is the matter?" the ghost asked again.

The memory of Tina's crestfallen face tugged at my subconscious.

I rubbed my face furiously and shook my head. "I let someone down yesterday. I shouldn't have."

The ghost cocked her head to one side thoughtfully. "Let us see another Christmas."

With a wave of her hand, the scene before us changed. My teenage self morphed into a twenty-one-year-old man. I was sitting on a low wall in the courtyard of my university. It was the last day of term, the ground adorned with festive decorations from a party the night before. On the wall beside me was Bella, my girlfriend at the time. She was crying.

This was a memory I'd rather not revisit.

"No, not this one," I pleaded. "Take me back."

"Hush," the ghost ordered.

"I thought you loved me," Bella said between sobs.

The young man next to her - me - pulled his arm away from her shoulders and his face hardened. "You did the right thing getting rid of it. We're too young; we're not ready to be parents."

"No!" Bella stood up quickly and glared at me. "You are not ready. You killed our baby."

She spun on her heel and ran away.

"Bella," both my young and present self called after her.

The ghost must have done that funky hand-waving thing while I was watching Bella's total dissolution. The image before me faded and it became the newspaper office. Drunk coworkers were photocopying various body parts amid a raucous Christmas party.

I was now in my thirties, excitedly talking to Tina.

"Maxwell just said I was a shoo-in for the promotion." My hands gesticulated wildly. "And it's because of you."

Tina squealed and flung her arms around my neck. "I'm so happy for you."

"What is going on here?" the ghost asked.

"My boss asked me to fix up the staff party. I didn't know how to organise something like that. Tina said she'd help." I paused to sweep my hand through the air at the joyous activities filling the office. "She made it amazing, but I got the pay rise..."

I trailed off remembering how she had never once begrudged my success. How genuine she had been.

"One more, I think." The ghost flicked her hand.

This time I was not in the image.

Tina was in a parked car outside her parents' house. A large tree decorated in flashing blue lights stood proudly in their front garden. Tina looked scared. Harry, the idiot she had dated eight years ago, glared at her from the driver's seat.

"Get out the car," he growled.

"Please, just five minutes. Come in, say hello, then go," she begged nervously.

"I'm not fucking playing happy families. I only agreed to drive you so you'd stay last night. Get out before I make you." He leaned closer to follow through on the threat.

I balled my fists.

"They are just images of consciousness. They can not see or hear us," the ghost said softly.

I loosened my tightly clasped hands and made no move towards the couple. Instead, I rubbed my jaw and sighed. I wanted to smash that smug twat's face for frightening Tina, but I had no reason to doubt the ghost telling me I couldn't intervene.

Tina got out dejectedly and reached for a bag in the back as the bastard revved the engine. He pulled away before she could shut the door. It swung a couple of times then slammed shut as he sped down the road.

She wiped her eyes and took a deep breath. Standing taller, she rolled her shoulders back, looking as if she was about to go into battle. The front door opened to reveal her mother.

"Come inside, it's cold." Tina's mum jumped when the fast disappearing car backfired. "Harry not able to stay?"

"Happy Christmas." Tina hugged her. "He has to get to his sister's."

"Maybe next year," her mum said looking wistful.

"Hopefully," Tina replied quietly as her mum steered them inside.

Anger built. No one treated my friends like that, especially no two-bit waste of space man. Unable to vent on the focus of my fury, I swung around to glare at the dwarf ghost.

"Enough," I snapped.

Her angelic face was shimmering, changing from youthful to haggard and back. Throughout the transitions, the glow persisted in a halo around her. I suddenly realized that damn halo held the power. I'm not sure why I knew that, but right then I could not be more sure of anything else. Whatever this tiny thing was, wrapped in my dressing gown, I wanted it gone.

Frustration boiled over, along with the myriad of emotions I had just suffered. My dead parents. My unborn child. The pain of Bella. Tina's fear. It was too much.

I didn't think, I just reached to claw at the side of the ghost's head. I tried to crush the light. The ghost resisted - if you could call it resisting. She slowly turned her head side to side and the light shafted around my fingers.

I needed to block the light. I stepped closer and threw my arms over the top of her head. I had no other option, except to smother the ghost.

"Take me home," I demanded.

The ghost flickered in my embrace, becoming smaller. The light faded into a soft glow and finally extinguished.

Utter exhaustion hit me like a tidal wave. Seeing I was in my room, with a welcoming bed, I curled up and fell into a deep sleep.

Chapter Three

Stave 3: The Second of the Three Spirits

A kiss awoke me. A soft sensual kiss. My eyes flickered open to see Kerry's plump, pouty, and flawless expression hovering over me. A picture that would be perfect for her latest Insta update.

"Morning, baby," I said, stretching my arms above my head, refreshed, my nightmares gone.

"Well yeah, I guess it is morning." Kerry laughed.

My eyes automatically flicked to the bedside clock. I groaned audibly. It was only one-thirty. Damn.

Kerry leaned closer, kissing me on the neck. She slowly trailed her lips downwards, pausing to lightly suck and tease my nipple - a body part many women ignore - but not her; she was the epitome of sensual seduction.

Her silky hair tickled my chest as she moved to give the same attention to my other nipple.

For no good reason, my eyes glanced at the clock again. What the hell? The minute digits were counting through time at an unearthly speed.

01:35

Kerry's tongue expertly swirled around my navel.

01:37

01:38

She gently massaged my abdominals. Teeth and lips playfully sucked and nipped.

01:40

01:41

Blood pooled in my groin.

Hands joined her tongue, stroking, and kneading my hips. Her hair continued to taunt my body.

01:47

01:48

Fuck no. No more.

I knew what was coming if I let her continue. My cock wilted at the memory of the excruciating pain. I must act now before she finally castrated me.

I sat up abruptly and caught her shoulders. She gasped then giggled as I smoothly flipped her over and I pinned her wrists either side of her head. I leaned down and kissed her forcefully.

It only took a moment for her to open her mouth and welcome me. Our tongues danced and explored. After I had had my fill I closed the kiss and shifted my weight enough to kiss her elegant neck. She moaned. By controlling her pleasure I felt confident I could stop the next spirit's arrival. I was no fool, if I didn't cum they would have no power over me.

I traced my tongue over the small implant scar under her arm before trailing kisses across the globe of her glorious breast. Her breathing deepened with each touch.

I permitted myself a glance at the clock as my lips found a hard nipple.

01:48

Good, it was working.

Kerry arched her back, begging with her whole body. I focused my attention on her other nipple, my fingers pinching and teasing the one I had just abandoned. She wound her hands into my hair, pulling me closer as I ran my teeth over the perky nub of flesh between my lips.

With her nipple in my mouth, I shifted my weight onto my elbow. Releasing the other breast I traced a hand lightly down her body, sweeping it back and forth to caress all the skin I could. I gently scraped my nails over her firm stomach and afford myself another time check.

01:48

Kerry spread her legs and pushed her hips a little off the bed. I released her nipple and kissed her again. She moaned into my mouth as my fingers teased her pussy lips. She was so wet I could feel her slick already. This was perfect; I didn't want time to move forward.

I slowly stroked along one puffy labium. Her legs spread wider, and her fingers found my shoulders as I continued down the other side. She vibrated and whimpered with need - it sounded divine.

With a single finger, I circled her engorged clit. She shifted her hips in a vain effort to move my touch to where she wanted it most.

Without a moment's hesitation, I plunged two fingers into her warm, wet cavern. Kerry yelped and thrust up to meet me, but I had already pulled my hand free. Bringing it upwards I broke the kiss and offered my soaked fingers to her luscious pout. She quickly opened her mouth. A delicate hand caught my wrist and pulled my digits in. Her tongue swirled and sucked them clean.

She finally let me go and I dipped my fingers into her drenched pussy again, though this time I let her watch as I tasted the juices myself.

"Fuck me, please fuck me," she begged.

01:48

No way, José, this wasn't about my pleasure. Whatever I was doing was working, only an idiot would've stopped.

Ignoring the pleas, I moved down the bed and between her spread legs. The scent that wafted up was intoxicating. I paused to enjoy the glistening folds.

"I need your cock. Just fuck me." She pushed her hips up.

My hands firmly gripped the inside of her thighs, holding her still. Not on your life, love. My cock was not coming out to play until well past two am. I dropped my face to her pussy. She bucked and cried out as a small orgasm rippled through her body from merely my touch.

Forcing myself to go slow I let my tongue glide up and down her lower lips. She quivered and groaned. I felt like a god. I nibbled and kissed, and smiled hearing her whimpers.

Spreading her lips with two fingers, my tongue circled her desperate clit. She might be a seductress but I was no naive virgin either. I'd studied sex and a woman's body with such gusto I'd probably have a Ph.D. if any university awarded them. In confirmation of my expertise, each time I grazed that engorged flesh another small orgasm shuddered through her.

Sensing she was at the edge of her tolerance I enclosed her clit and feasted. I sucked as she screamed. I moved down a little and pushed my tongue into her pussy. The walls tightened and pulsed around me as I drove deeper. The air filled with cries of ecstasy as her orgasms continued to mount in a crescendo.

Returning to her clit I massaged it with my tongue. The space allowed me to slide two fingers inside her soaked pussy. Turning my hand, muscle memory alone found the spongy area I sought. Hooking upwards, I worked her G-spot in time with my relentless tongue.

Kerry sobbed in bliss. Wetness sprayed out, coating my face. Glorious, the taste was glorious. I'm addicted to a woman's cum.

She was in one long, incoherent orgasm as I heard Big Ben ring out a chime. The fluid continued to spray as she came harder. I drank all I could, savouring each drop like nectar.

Satiated, I went to pull back, but her thighs closed like a vice around my head. Fuck, this was hot.

I lapped up her squirt and continued to thrust my fingers. She shook, screamed, and bucked never letting my head go.

Okay, I was starting to need oxygen. As incredible as it was to be the cause of the hysterical girl's ecstasy I was feeling woozy. All those gym workouts to maintain her figure had given Kerry surprisingly strong thighs. Weakness made my pumping fingers stop and slip out of her pulsating cunt, yet still, she came. I was drowning in the continual squirt.

Fuck! This is what dying of water torture must be like.

The second chime of Big Ben rang out.

Unable to breathe I lost consciousness.

Chapter Four

With a sob, air dragged through my starved lungs. Immediately, I was wide awake and sitting up.

Ready.

I gripped the blanket under me and scanned the room. My whole body on edge, as I searched for the danger I knew lurked in my room.

Nothing.

Huh?

My room was still... well... my room. Kerry was missing but everything else was the same. The bedside light emitted a low glow; heavy curtains concealed the window, and my clothes lay neatly folded on the bucket chair.

I sighed with relief and scanned the room again. That's when I noticed the light seeping under the door. I didn't leave the living room light on. *Did I?* Curiosity may have killed the cat, but I didn't want to waste electricity. I got up and cautiously moved towards the door, half expecting a monster's hand to grab me from under the bed. But nothing happened.

I slowly opened the door.

The sight that greeted me made me gasp and step back.

Two small children sat on my living room floor, between them was a large pile of Lego bricks. The slightly taller child, a girl, studied a sheet of instructions, describing a colour and shape to the smaller boy. He rooted around in the pile then held up a tiny piece of Lego, making the girl squeal with joy.

It looked like a happy textbook Christmas morning scene, confirmed by the large, brightly decorated tree proudly filling the corner of the room. But what the fuck were they doing in my apartment?

A snore made me jump. It came from a yellow Labrador sleeping against the radiator. The dog's tail lazily thumped as it dreamed of chasing rabbits across open fields.

"Kids, sing with me," a woman's voice called from the direction of my kitchen.

She sounded familiar, but before I could work out who it was, the sound of Mariah Carey flooded the room as a radio was turned up. The two children started singing loudly and the unseen woman joined in. The cacophony of noise didn't let me decipher the voice enough to identify who she was.

I stepped into my living room, unnoticed by the merry children. A pleasant smell of cinnamon and sage wafted through the air. Moving towards the kitchen I was so focused on finding out whose Christmas I had invaded I almost walked into a rather large man who suddenly appeared before me.

I stumbled, only stopped from falling by landing on the arm of the sofa. I lifted my head to look up at the imposing figure.

What I assumed was the second ghost smiled down at me. He had a jovial round face and ruddy cheeks, a wreath of holly sat on his head. He was clothed in a long dark red robe with white fur lining the collar and cuffs. As peculiar as he looked, for a giant of a man, he seemed quite friendly.

"I am-"

I held up my hand to cut him off. "Christmas Present. I know. I know. I have read the book and watched the films."

"Hold my robe," he replied with a chuckle.

Now if a giant appears in your apartment, and that very same apartment has been invaded by a model 2.4 family - with a dog - you tell me if you'd refuse that giant's order? In case you're wondering, I didn't either.

The moment my hand touched the soft red material I was outside flying through the air. Clearly, my dreams were not coherent as this appeared to have become The Snowman. I half expected Aled Jones to start singing about walking in the air.

We raced through the cool crisp air, though I didn't feel cold. Below us, the city was eerily quiet. Roads normally filled with frustrated commuters were empty. Office buildings stood in darkness with none of the usual bustling activities.

The giant changed direction and headed towards Hyde Park. He took us lower and I closed my eyes, ready for what I was sure would be a fatal impact. Instead, we landed lightly on our feet. I quickly took stock of my limbs to confirm nothing was broken. Satisfied I was unhurt, I looked up.

A few feet away a man was holding the back of a bicycle. On the bike sat a young boy, his face studious with effort as his small feet turned the pedals. The man jogged behind, giving lots of encouragement. Their combined speed increased and the man let go and stood watching the child wobble away.

"Yes, Dexter, yes, keep going," he yelled after the bike.

"I did it," the child squealed before unceremoniously falling over.

In a split second the man was by his side.

"Daddy, I did it," the boy said triumphantly, as his father gathered him in his arms, hugging him tightly.

"Mum's going to be so impressed." The father put the child down and stood the bike up. "Let's see if you can do it again, and I'll film it so you can send it to Nana."

I smiled watching them.

A rustle of material made me look at the giant. His hair had grown grey under the holly crown and his stomach appeared to be larger. He took a step towards the man and child then we were in the air again. The giant rummaged in his robe and pulled out a handful of what looked like glitter. He sprinkled it on the father and son as we passed over.

With exceptional speed, we flew out of the city towards the sprawling suburbs and landed on a driveway. A woman in a gaudy penguin sweater was packing a car with brightly coloured bags filled with festively wrapped presents. A man came out of the house carrying a baby in one of those car-cot-things. He kissed the woman on the cheek then put the baby in its little safe holder on the back seat of the car.

I glanced at the ghost expecting an explanation. I got none. He had grown older, a grey beard was emerging over his chin, and he was fatter. He threw more glitter towards the family and their car.

In the air again, we raced over a vast ocean. Even at the speed we were travelling I could see dolphins jumping and dancing below us. The giant chuckled watching them too.

Our next landing was in a military base. A man in fatigues was grinning at a computer. I moved behind him and saw a young girl waving out of the screen. The soldier waved back.

"Have you been a good girl?" he asked.

"Yes, Daddy, yes. Look what Santa got me." The girl brightly held up a new iPhone. She frowned. "But he didn't bring me you."

"I know, baby." The man touched the screen. "But I'll be home soon and we will have a second Christmas when I do."

The girl's face lit up. "With more presents?"

The soldier laughed and nodded. "With more presents."

The girl, in some country thousands of miles away, leaned forward and kissed the camera, turning the screen black.

A strange warmth filled my gut as I observed the touching scene before me.

The jolly ghost threw a double handful of glitter at the man.

Chapter Five

Across more oceans, mountains and deserts we flew. The ghost slipped through a small window taking me with him. Considering he had grown rounder, and older he was surprisingly nimble for a giant. His beard was thick and white, and as imposing as his frame was, he blended seamlessly into the corner of the cramped room we stood in.

On the bed was a naked man who, in post-coltial exhaustion, had collapsed over a slim woman. I'm fairly open-minded and nonjudgmental but voyeurism isn't one of my personal kinks. I looked up at the ghost chuckling beside me. He put a finger to his lips silencing me before I could share my disgust at snooping on the amorous couple.

The man disengaged his spent cock and rolled on to his back, to reveal the very relaxed face of the young woman he had just well-fucked. It was an expression I knew well.

He reached under the bed and pulled out a small, carefully wrapped box. Scanning the tiny room, with the barely functional small kitchenette in the corner, I strongly suspected under the bed was the only storage he had.

"Tom, no, we said no presents this year while we're saving for a deposit." The woman still took the gift he offered.

"This is important." He kissed her on the lips. "Merry Christmas."

She hurriedly tore the paper then lifted the lid on the box. Her hand flew to her mouth as her eyes flashed from him to the box and back.

The man - still stark bollock naked - jumped out of the bed and knelt on the floor beside her. He took her hand and drew it to touch it with his lips.

"Miss Hassler, would you do me the great honour of becoming Mrs. Cowan?" he asked, his eyes sparkling with hope and love.

The woman sobbed and nodded.

He gently took the ring out of the box and slipped it onto her finger. "This is just for now. If I get that job I'll get you a better one."

"It's perfect. I love it." She turned the cheap ring, then

kissed him passionately. "I don't want a different one, I just want you."

He laughed and pushed her back onto the bed.

A double handful of glitter drifted over the couple as we flew out of the small window.

The ghost continued to transport me from one happy Christmas scene to another. We visited many countries and people. At each place, I witnessed love and joy. We were unseen and uninvited intruders on strangers deeply touching and private Christmas moments.

The shadows had grown long as the sun lowered in the sky, giving way to darkness when we arrived back in London.

The ghost now bore a thick white beard and his grey hair was curling over his shoulders. He was almost as round as he was tall and the red robe strained over his expanding gut. He stood, surprisingly neatly considering his size, in the doorway of a detached house.

A couple my age were swaying together to the sounds of Michael Bublé. They slowly turned and I realised the woman was Bella, older, but still unmistakably her. She was sobbing quietly on the man's shoulder as he held her.

"Honey, it's okay. Next time will be our time," he said, stroking her back.

She pulled away from his embrace and looked at the floor.

"What if it's my fault? What if this is karma for killing my baby?" she mumbled.

"No. I will not let you say that." He caught her chin with a finger and gently lifted her face so she was looking at him. "He made you do it. If there is karma, that bastard Ebenezer is the one who will get bitten on the arse."

The hairs on the back of my neck stood up. His prediction was a little too close to home.

"But we've been trying for months and it still hasn't happened," Bella said sorrowfully.

He smiled at her. "And we will try for as many months as it takes."

She opened her mouth to speak but he stopped her by lightly resting a finger over her lips.

"Danny told me about this place. A clinic in Turkey. If we're not pregnant by the spring, let's investigate it a bit more."

Bella smiled under his finger.

"He said that's how his Mrs got their twins."

"I love you." Bella kissed his finger as the ghost threw what looked like a whole bucket of glitter over them.

"Why do some get more of that stuff than others?" I asked nodding towards the sparkling cloud floating around Bella and her partner.

"The ones who have hope even in the face of adversity?" The jolly rosy faced ghost smiled down at me.

'Yes. The soldier, the poor couple." I looked wistfully

towards Bella who was back slowly dancing with the man. "Precious Bella. Tell me, will she get her baby?"

"I've been around over two thousand years. I bring happiness. Now we must go."

This was the only answer I would be getting as we took to the air. Much more used to this mode of travel now, I could tell we were heading north from the motorways webbed below us.

I recognised the house before we landed. It was Tina's parents home again. I followed the ghost into the lounge.

Tina, looking tired, sat on the sofa next to her mother.

"I don't understand why Ebb didn't come."

"Mum, we were never together; it was for show," Tina said, exasperated.

"But seven years he's been with you." Her mum scowled. "Why have you split up?"

"We haven't, we are just friends. He came here to stop you asking what was wrong with me for, not being married."

"You dated other men but you brought him, not them?" Her mum shook her head confused. "Why not bring your actual boyfriend?"

Tina put her face in her hands. "None of them were good enough to introduce you to."

"Well, Ebb can't be very good either then."

My jaw tightened.

Tina's eyes blazed with anger. "He is a good man."

I smiled at her feistiness.

"I always thought he was a wrong 'un, him and Marley got on far too well," her mum continued, ignoring Tina's frustration.

"Ebb's an acquired taste, but he is my friend. A good one, a hide-the-body one."

"Huh?" Her mum furrowed her brow.

My smile turned into a wicked grin. Yes, I was her hide-the-body friend.

"The sort of friend if I rang up and said I've killed someone, would tell me he was on his way with a shovel to help me hide it." Tina smiled, and her eyes glinted. "And he wouldn't ask any questions."

Her mum cocked her head to the side. "If you're so determined to create a happy facade to fool me and your father, then why is he not here if he is such a good friend?"

I swallowed hard. Guilt was, not an emotion I experienced often, but her mum was right.

Tina lost her smile. "He got a better offer."

Before her mum could reply, Tina's niece, Rosie, came in and caught her hand and pulled her off the sofa.

Tina went willingly. At the dining room table, a game of Pie Face had been set up. Thankfully, the interrogation about my absence faded. The extended family laughed and screamed until each person had had a face full of spray cream unceremoniously splattered over them.

I found myself laughing when a large glob of cream landed on Tina's nose and she tried, in vain, to lick it off.

There was a pause in the festivities when the family watched the Queen's speech then more games and raucous fun followed.

I was genuinely enjoying myself, I even shouted out unheard answers during a game of charades. So immersed I forgot about my giant companion, it felt like I was part of the happiness filling the home. Remembering I wasn't alone I looked over to see the ghost was much older and he looked tired. His massive stomach moved and twitched under the straining robes.

"What's with that?" I asked, nodding towards the shape, shifting out of sight.

The ghost unwrapped the red cloth and withdrew two children, which he dropped at his feet.

I recognized them and gasped. They were the small boy and girl I had seen in my apartment earlier, but they had changed. No longer vibrant, happy kids, they were now starved and dressed in dull rags. The children curled in a fetal position at the giant's feet. I stepped back in horror.

"What have you done to them?" I demanded.

"You did it. They are yours," he said solemnly.

"No. Make them whole again, sprinkle that glitter crap on them."

"The boy is Ignorance and the girl is Want." He looked down at the pitiful mites shivering on the ground.

"They need help, we need to take them to a hospital or social services." I crouched to look at the children closer.

"Beware the boy, for on his forehead I see written a Doom. If it is not erased it is yours to bear for eternity."

"I don't understand." I looked up pleadingly with the whimpers of the children beside me.

A clock began to chime. With each chime, the ghost grew older and wearier.

"Tell me what I must do." I tried to gather up the girl, but my hands passed through her translucent flesh. Panic engulfed me.

The clock struck twelve.

Stave 4: The Last of the Spirits

The last chime of Big Ben vibrated and I found myself back in my room. Kerry was softly snoring, curled under the blanket beside me. I rubbed a hand across my face and nearly took my eye out with the holly wreath I clutched.

Damn.

I looked at the holly. I smelt it. I even tested it was real by carefully biting it. The pre-decorated, minimalist, silver tree I had grudgingly put in the lounge didn't contain any holly so maybe the dream had happened.

I thought it was a vivid nightmare or at very least a hallucination. I'll admit when I was watching Tina and her family it had seemed real; I had been part of their festive spirit. But now I was sitting in my bed - at home - it had just gone midnight and Christmas Day had begun... again.

I shivered, remembering Marley's words - plus endless remakes of Dickens's story. I still had another phantom to come. I had best be ready.

The bedside clock turned through the minutes at what I considered a normal pace, but I didn't let my guard down. I stayed alert, searching for the next monster. With Kerry asleep and no sexual shenanigans, I hoped the ghost couldn't find me. Not that I relaxed or let my eyes droop for one minute.

Time crawled onwards. Big Ben chimed at one o'clock. My head ached and my shoulders burned with tension. Two o'clock rang out. Kerry was in such a deep sleep she remained blissfully unaware of my nighttime vigil. Her only contribution was occasional mumbles and snores from under the blanket.

The first chime of three made me catch my breath. I couldn't hold it long enough; I gasped once and held it again for the second ring. I repeated my actions when the third echoed outside.

Silence.

I slowly let my breath out.

Nothing.

No Marley in bondage, no grotesque dwarf by my bed, no unearthly glow under my door. Not quite ready to drop my guard, I let the digital clock count through another five minutes. Still, no phantom came.

My shoulders relaxed and I rolled them to release the knots in the tired muscles. My eyelids were so heavy. I needed to sleep. Setting the holly on the bedside stand I shuffled down the bed and spooned behind Kerry. She murmured and scooted back. She felt lovely, so warm. It was a nightmare - just a silly bad dream.

The girl in my arms yawned and turned to face me.

What the fuck?

I was out of the bed at the speed of light with my back hard up against the wall. I shook violently.

Kerry - or at least some repulsive caricature of her - sat up, letting the blanket pool at her waist. Her face was expressionless, the skin drawn back and stretched. Her cheeks were unnaturally full, like a greedy hamster wearing blusher. But the most striking thing about her face was the lips. They had become massively plump in a giant, cartoonish trout pout. I don't think the poor girl could have spoken even if she tried. Far bigger than the lips were her breasts. They sat high on her chest and extended in front of her at least a foot. Below the deformed boobs her waist was so tiny I could've wrapped my hands around it and had excess room.

Her expressionless eyes fixed on me as she swung her legs out of bed and stood up. Her pubic hair was dyed silver and gold with jewels reflecting in the low light of the bedside lamp. I think the hair was trimmed in a heart shape, but I honestly couldn't be sure as the shadow of her inflated breasts made clarification difficult and I wasn't going to get closer to... that thing.

She pointed at me with a dangerously long but perfectly manicured nail. Turning her hand she beckoned.

Fuck.

My legs trembled. Kerry - or what was once her - moved closer. The very air around her crackled with artificial, shallow fakeness. I dropped to my knees and bowed my head. You'd think I'd be used to being around ghosts by now, but trust me I wasn't. For all that had gone before her, this one I feared the most.

"Are you the Ghost of Christmases Not Yet Happened?" I asked through loudly chattering teeth.

She nodded her head slowly, not a flicker of an expression on her plastic face.

My skin crawled. I massaged my jaw with a shaking hand. Was this what Marley had meant when he said he had been by my side many days since he died? Had I been screwing a ghost? Had I been fucking Marley?

"Were you ever real?" I waited for a reaction, any reaction. "Can't you speak?"

She shook her head slowly. The fillers and Botox made it impossible for her face to move.

"You're going to show me shadows of the future." I rubbed my eyes, dreading her reply.

She pointed her manicured finger at the ground.

With a loud gulp I decided the sooner I got this over with, the better.

"Look I've met all of Marley's clan, but you really give me the creeps. I've learned my lesson. I know you're here to help me and I will go with you, but do you think we can do this quickly?"

Plastic Kerry tilted her flawless face and pursed her fat lips.

"Do you want some clothes before we go?" I asked, though I doubted any clothes would go over those ginormous breasts.

She curled her finger and the blanket levitated towards her. It wrapped itself over her head and around her body like a shroud.

Guessing we were set to go, I followed as she, rather boring and earthly like, walked through the doorway. Stepping out of my apartment building it was Christmas morning again. Families and couples bustled along the street, heading to meals of excess.

We stopped beside an elegant and attractive woman in her forties or maybe early fifties. She was talking to a more comely, plumper lady.

"They said he won't ever come home," the attractive lady said, setting a hold-all down at their feet.

"So you've just taken his stuff?"

"Only the valuable things." The first lady lifted a Rolex watch out of the bag.

"Isn't that like stealing from the dead?" the other woman asked, crouching to remove a smartphone from the bag.

"He isn't going to need it where he's going. Anyway, if I don't take it I'm sure one of his other women would." She took the phone and tapped in a passcode and turned it to show her companion. "Over 800 contacts and only a few are work related, the rest are women. This is his black book."

"And now it's yours."

Both women laughed.

I frowned, really hoping they were not talking about me. They couldn't be, they were far too old for either to be one of my conquests.

"Um... Kerry." I wasn't quite sure what to call the mute ghost. "Okay, I understand. If I don't change I could have ex-partners rooting through my personal effects like the poor sod those witches are cackling about."

The blanket covered ghost just pointed at the women.

"Show me someone who gives a damn about the schmuck these ladies are talking about, please," I said plaintively. Somebody must care about him.

With a swirl of the blanket shroud, I was back in my apartment. Tina sat hunched over, on my sofa. I - as a slightly older man - paced the room in front of her. Phew, I was still alive. I looked at my older self, pleased the speckling of silver hair made me look distinguished but not aged.

"I'll kill him," Tina growled, not looking up.

"Then why didn't you walk away sooner?" I watched myself stop and turn to face her. "Where is your anger and strength when you need it? You always do this." I crouched in front of her. "Every single time you let these bastards treat you like trash. Later - much much later - you come to me and show me your resilience, but you never show them."

Tina looked up, revealing a swollen and blackened eye. "I don't know."

"Tina, Tina, what am I going to do with you? How can I help?" my older self said in a singsong voice, as if I was talking to a child.

"Please phone my mum and tell her I'm sick so won't be able to drive up later. Please."

My heart went out to her. My older self sat down and put his arm around her shoulders.

She rested her head on my chest and I caught a muffled, "Thank you."

"So it was me those women stole from?" I asked the

ghost. This timeline appeared to not be following a chronological order.

She swirled her blanket cape and I was back at Tina's parents' house.

"It's your fault," her father shouted at her mother.

"John, how can you say that?" Tina's mum had red puffy eyes.

"You never let her be, always pushing and demanding she find a husband." John glared at his wife.

"I wanted her to be happy." Her mum put her head in her hands. "I loved her, I wanted her to be happy."

"You drove her straight into his arms... and fists. It is your fault," John spat back.

"What...what's happened to Tina?" I nervously looked at the ghost.

She pointed that fucking annoying manicured hand towards the door.

I ran in that direction, desperate to know where Tina was.

Outside was no longer their front lawn and driveway. I was in a graveyard.

I swallowed uncomfortably.

Please, no. Please, no.

A new headstone stood by a pile of freshly turned earth, which was covered in brightly colored flowers.

Much as I dreaded what I would see, I moved closer to the stone and read the inscription.

Katrina Hopkins

Much loved daughter, sister and friend.

Taken too soon.

1983-2036

"No! No! No!" I shouted at the grave then swung around to stare in disbelief at the ghost. "Why didn't I stop it? I would've saved her."

The ghost swirled her blanket.

We were in some sort of care facility. An orderly was pushing a grey-haired, shriveled man in a wheelchair. They were moving away from us, but I could see the man was hunched over and drooling.

"Turkey soup today," the orderly merrily told his patient.

They turned a corner letting me see the man's face. I recoiled in horror. It was me.

The orderly pulled a flimsy paper crown out of his pocket and put it on my living-dead head.

"What happened? Tell me?" I demanded.

The ghost pushed the blanket cloak off her head. Kerry, with the surgically deformed face, stared blandly.

You had a stroke. Stress and excess. The aneurysm starved your brain of oxygen. Her overly filled lips did not move and no sound came out, but I heard every word. Telepathic fucking ghosts - yeah, I should've expected that.

My whole body shook. "I've learned my lesson. Please I want to find true happiness. I can change the future."

I lunged forward to grasp her hand, catching myself on the red talons. She tried to pull free, but I clung on - my life depended on it.

"The past, present and future you've all shown me. I won't be selfish. I want the hope of the things I can be part of."

Kerry snatched her hand back and I fell on to the ground.

"I want to share my love, and feel the love of others," I sobbed at her feet. "I have hope."

The blanket slipped off her modified body. I sat back on my heels with my mouth open. She shimmered, becoming translucent, and finally faded and shrank into my bucket chair.

Chapter Six

Stave 4: The Last of the Spirits

The last chime of Big Ben vibrated and I found myself back in my room. Kerry was softly snoring, curled under the blanket beside me. I rubbed a hand across my face and nearly took my eye out with the holly wreath I clutched.

Damn.

I looked at the holly. I smelt it. I even tested it was real by carefully biting it. The pre-decorated, minimalist, silver tree I had grudgingly put in the lounge didn't contain any holly so maybe the dream had happened.

I thought it was a vivid nightmare or at very least a hallucination. I'll admit when I was watching Tina and her family it had seemed real; I had been part of their festive spirit. But now I was sitting in my bed - at home - it had just gone midnight and Christmas Day had begun... again.

I shivered, remembering Marley's words - plus endless remakes of Dickens's story. I still had another phantom to come. I had best be ready.

The bedside clock turned through the minutes at what I considered a normal pace, but I didn't let my guard down. I stayed alert, searching for the next monster. With Kerry asleep and no sexual shenanigans, I hoped the ghost couldn't find me. Not that I relaxed or let my eyes droop for one minute.

Time crawled onwards. Big Ben chimed at one o'clock. My head ached and my shoulders burned with tension. Two o'clock rang out. Kerry was in such a deep sleep she remained blissfully unaware of my nighttime vigil. Her only contribution was occasional mumbles and snores from under the blanket.

The first chime of three made me catch my breath. I couldn't hold it long enough; I gasped once and held it again for the second ring. I repeated my actions when the third echoed outside.

Silence.

I slowly let my breath out.

Nothing.

No Marley in bondage, no grotesque dwarf by my bed, no unearthly glow under my door. Not quite ready to drop my guard, I let the digital clock count through another five minutes. Still, no phantom came.

My shoulders relaxed and I rolled them to release the knots in the tired muscles. My eyelids were so heavy. I needed to sleep. Setting the holly on the bedside stand I shuffled down the bed and spooned behind Kerry. She murmured and scooted back. She felt lovely, so warm. It was a nightmare - just a silly bad dream.

The girl in my arms yawned and turned to face me.

What the fuck?

I was out of the bed at the speed of light with my back hard up against the wall. I shook violently.

Kerry - or at least some repulsive caricature of her - sat up, letting the blanket pool at her waist. Her face was expressionless, the skin drawn back and stretched. Her cheeks were unnaturally full, like a greedy hamster wearing blusher. But the most striking thing about her face was the lips. They had become massively plump in a giant, cartoonish trout pout. I don't think the poor girl could have spoken even if she tried. Far bigger than the lips were her breasts. They sat high on her chest and extended in front of her at least a foot. Below the deformed boobs her waist was so tiny I could've wrapped my hands around it and had excess room.

Her expressionless eyes fixed on me as she swung her legs out of bed and stood up. Her pubic hair was dyed silver and gold with jewels reflecting in the low light of the bedside lamp. I think the hair was trimmed in a heart shape, but I honestly couldn't be sure as the shadow of her inflated breasts made clarification difficult and I wasn't going to get closer to... that thing.

She pointed at me with a dangerously long but perfectly manicured nail. Turning her hand she beckoned.

Fuck.

My legs trembled. Kerry - or what was once her - moved closer. The very air around her crackled with artificial, shallow fakeness. I dropped to my knees and bowed my head. You'd think I'd be used to being around ghosts by now, but trust me I wasn't. For all that had gone before her, this one I feared the most.

"Are you the Ghost of Christmases Not Yet Happened?" I asked through loudly chattering teeth.

She nodded her head slowly, not a flicker of an expression on her plastic face.

My skin crawled. I massaged my jaw with a shaking hand. Was this what Marley had meant when he said he had been by my side many days since he died? Had I been screwing a ghost? Had I been fucking Marley?

"Were you ever real?" I waited for a reaction, any reaction. "Can't you speak?"

She shook her head slowly. The fillers and Botox made it impossible for her face to move.

"You're going to show me shadows of the future." I rubbed my eyes, dreading her reply.

She pointed her manicured finger at the ground.

With a loud gulp I decided the sooner I got this over with, the better.

"Look I've met all of Marley's clan, but you really give me the creeps. I've learned my lesson. I know you're here to help me and I will go with you, but do you think we can do this quickly?"

Plastic Kerry tilted her flawless face and pursed her fat lips.

"Do you want some clothes before we go?" I asked, though I doubted any clothes would go over those ginormous breasts.

She curled her finger and the blanket levitated towards her. It wrapped itself over her head and around her body like a shroud.

Guessing we were set to go, I followed as she, rather boring and earthly like, walked through the doorway. Stepping out of my apartment building it was Christmas morning again. Families and couples bustled along the street, heading to meals of excess.

We stopped beside an elegant and attractive woman in her forties or maybe early fifties. She was talking to a more comely, plumper lady.

"They said he won't ever come home," the attractive lady said, setting a hold-all down at their feet.

"So you've just taken his stuff?"

"Only the valuable things." The first lady lifted a Rolex watch out of the bag.

"Isn't that like stealing from the dead?" the other woman asked, crouching to remove a smartphone from the bag.

"He isn't going to need it where he's going. Anyway, if I don't take it I'm sure one of his other women would." She took the phone and tapped in a passcode and turned it to show her companion. "Over 800 contacts and only a few are work related, the rest are women. This is his black book."

"And now it's yours."

Both women laughed.

I frowned, really hoping they were not talking about me. They couldn't be, they were far too old for either to be one of my conquests.

"Um... Kerry." I wasn't quite sure what to call the mute ghost. "Okay, I understand. If I don't change I could have ex-partners rooting through my personal effects like the poor sod those witches are cackling about."

The blanket covered ghost just pointed at the women.

"Show me someone who gives a damn about the schmuck these ladies are talking about, please," I said plaintively. Somebody must care about him.

With a swirl of the blanket shroud, I was back in my

apartment. Tina sat hunched over, on my sofa. I - as a slightly older man - paced the room in front of her. Phew, I was still alive. I looked at my older self, pleased the speckling of silver hair made me look distinguished but not aged.

"I'll kill him," Tina growled, not looking up.

"Then why didn't you walk away sooner?" I watched myself stop and turn to face her. "Where is your anger and strength when you need it? You always do this." I crouched in front of her. "Every single time you let these bastards treat you like trash. Later - much much later - you come to me and show me your resilience, but you never show them."

Tina looked up, revealing a swollen and blackened eye. "I don't know."

"Tina, Tina, what am I going to do with you? How can I help?" my older self said in a singsong voice, as if I was talking to a child.

"Please phone my mum and tell her I'm sick so won't be able to drive up later. Please."

My heart went out to her. My older self sat down and put his arm around her shoulders.

She rested her head on my chest and I caught a muffled, "Thank you."

"So it was me those women stole from?" I asked the ghost. This timeline appeared to not be following a chronological order.

She swirled her blanket cape and I was back at Tina's parents' house.

"It's your fault," her father shouted at her mother.

"John, how can you say that?" Tina's mum had red puffy eyes.

"You never let her be, always pushing and demanding she find a husband." John glared at his wife.

"I wanted her to be happy." Her mum put her head in her hands. "I loved her, I wanted her to be happy."

"You drove her straight into his arms... and fists. It is your fault," John spat back.

"What...what's happened to Tina?" I nervously looked at the ghost.

She pointed that fucking annoying manicured hand towards the door.

I ran in that direction, desperate to know where Tina was.

Outside was no longer their front lawn and driveway. I was in a graveyard.

I swallowed uncomfortably.

Please, no. Please, no.

A new headstone stood by a pile of freshly turned earth, which was covered in brightly colored flowers.

Much as I dreaded what I would see, I moved closer to the stone and read the inscription.

Katrina Hopkins

Much loved daughter, sister and friend.

Taken too soon.

1983-2036

"No! No! No!" I shouted at the grave then swung around to stare in disbelief at the ghost. "Why didn't I stop it? I would've saved her."

The ghost swirled her blanket.

We were in some sort of care facility. An orderly was pushing a grey-haired, shriveled man in a wheelchair. They were moving away from us, but I could see the man was hunched over and drooling.

"Turkey soup today," the orderly merrily told his patient.

They turned a corner letting me see the man's face. I recoiled in horror. It was me.

The orderly pulled a flimsy paper crown out of his pocket and put it on my living-dead head.

"What happened? Tell me?" I demanded.

The ghost pushed the blanket cloak off her head. Kerry, with the surgically deformed face, stared blandly.

You had a stroke. Stress and excess. The aneurysm starved your brain of oxygen. Her overly filled lips did not move and no sound came out, but I heard every word. Telepathic fucking ghosts - yeah, I should've expected that.

My whole body shook. "I've learned my lesson. Please I want to find true happiness. I can change the future."

I lunged forward to grasp her hand, catching myself

on the red talons. She tried to pull free, but I clung on - my life depended on it.

"The past, present and future you've all shown me. I won't be selfish. I want the hope of the things I can be part of."

Kerry snatched her hand back and I fell on to the ground.

"I want to share my love, and feel the love of others," I sobbed at her feet. "I have hope."

The blanket slipped off her modified body. I sat back on my heels with my mouth open. She shimmered, becoming translucent, and finally faded and shrank into my bucket chair.

Chapter Seven

Stave 5: The End of It

Yes!

I scrambled out of bed.

The chair was mine. The room was mine. The time was mine to change. I had survived Marley and his three ghosts.

I picked up the wreath of holly and held it aloft. It wasn't a dream.

"Marley, I won't forget. I have hope," I shouted out to my empty room.

I felt as light as a feather, as joyful as a lamb, as happy as a drunk, as giddy as a virgin getting his first lay. I threw my clothes on, grabbed a warm coat and keys and set off. I had so much to do and so little time.

Thank Santa, it was Christmas Day and the police

were notably absent this early. I drove quickly through the almost deserted streets of the city, with the sun just starting to rise. I already knew it would be a cold, crisp day, just as the ghost of Christmas Present had shown me.

The guy in the newsagent wished me a Merry Christmas when I burst in to buy a bunch of flowers and a congratulations card. I suspect he thought I was a failed husband purchasing a feeble gift to pacify a forgotten guest. Ignoring his look of consternation, I grinned like the cat who got the cream and wished him well.

Back in my car, it took me a little longer to locate the council block, but with some stop-starting and backtracking, I found my destination. Parking, I looked up at the high rise and counted the windows, amazed I'd managed to recollect the details.

The communal area stank of urine as I made my way up the concrete steps. Luckily for me, only two rooms on the fourth floor appeared to be occupied; the other doors stood barricaded up. The moans and cries coming from behind one door made me confident this was the place. I put all the cash I had on me into the card and sealed the envelope. I propped the flowers against the door before sliding the card under the door.

"Miss Hassler, would you do me the great honour of becoming Mrs Cowan?" muffled words came through the door.

The accompanying squeal and sob made me smile as I took the steps two at a time back down to my car.

* * *

I managed to reach the park as the man and young boy on the bike went past.

"He's doing great," I said, still a little breathless from my mad dash.

"I know." The father beamed back. "My wife said he was too young, but I knew he was ready."

"Let me film you both," I offered.

The man got his phone out. "Merry Christmas, and thank you."

They were strangers yet they felt like old friends. I laughed and cheered watching the boy master his bike. After a few minutes, I reluctantly left them but chuckled to myself knowing one day I'd be teaching my own son to ride a bike. Excited at the prospect I went to my office. I needed some help with my next endeavor and I was on a tight schedule to get to hers on time.

I stepped back surprised when Tina's neighbour, Mary, opened the door. In her arms was a large, brightly colored, wrapped box.

"Oh, hello, Ebb. Merry Christmas," she said, looking suspiciously from my head to my feet and back up. "Tina's not here."

I narrowed my eyes at the young woman. For an intruder stealing gifts, she didn't seem very guilty.

"She said I could hide Sammy's scooter here. She gave me a key before she left." She awkwardly squeezed herself and the box through the door.

"Left when?" I took the box and let her lock the door.

"Last night." She scowled at me. "You know it's Christmas. Are you okay? You look a bit strange."

Damn, I'd missed her.

"Yeah, yeah, gotta go." I paused my escape to look back. "Merry Christmas, Sammy will love the scooter."

"Bye, Santa," she called after me, laughing.

* * *

"Happy Christmas, Ebb," Tina said, answering the phone. "Didn't expect you to call with Kerry over."

"She doesn't exist," I said, negotiating my way onto the motorway.

"What? You okay? Sounds like I'm on handsfree. Where's Kerry?" Her voice had a nervous edge.

"Don't worry, there's no body to hide." I chuckled.

"Where is Kerry?" she asked again, not missing a beat.

"She's not real."

"Are you driving drunk?"

"Drunk on life." I put the BMW into top gear.

"Ebb, I need you to breathe and tell me what's happened. Where is Kerry?" Tina spoke slowly and deliberately.

"She was just in my head. She never existed."

"You made her up to avoid coming to my parents?" Even with the distortion of the car speakers, she sounded hurt.

"No, no, I thought she was real. I've had an epiphany. Tina, I'm coming."

"You've been talking about her for weeks. I don't understand... coming where?" The hurt tone was replaced by confusion.

"To you, I'm about two hours away." I changed lanes to pass a milk tanker.

"Kerry?"

"Have you ever met her?" I asked.

"No."

"Have I ever shown any photos of her?"

"No." She sighed. "I still don't understand."

"Tell your mum I'm coming for lunch." I cut the call off before she could reply.

I cancelled the call when Tina rang back and shuddered remembering Kerry. I'd met her outside a coffee shop and thinking back I never saw her interact with anyone except me. Enamored by this exquisite girl coming on to me, I hadn't been about to object when our relationship had been purely sex and nothing more. I swallowed hard. The idea my cock had been buried - many times - in the ghost of my future, made me nauseous.

I turned my phone off when Tina rang again.

Chapter Eight

Tina had the door open before I clumsily got out of the car. Hands on her hips she watched me retrieve a sack from the passenger seat.

"Merry Christmas" I cheerily called. "You look great."

She glanced down at her reindeer sweater and looked back at me.

"Why are you dressed as Santa Claus?" She shook her head to hide the smile. "And how did you get a Santa outfit?"

"Borrowed it from the office."

I dropped the sack at our feet and gathered her into a warm embrace. The red nose on the reindeer squeaked when I crushed it with the stomach padding of my costume. She laughed in my arms.

"I don't know why you're here. In fact, I'm not sure I

want to know. But it's good to see you," she mumbled into my chest.

I held her tight. Damn, she felt good. She was alive; I can't tell you how happy it made me knowing she was alive. I dropped a kiss on the top of her head.

"The why is because I wanted to see you." I rested my chin on her head just enjoying hugging her. "Have you told your mum we're not together?"

"No, not yet. Said last week I didn't think you'd be able to come; she hasn't interrogated me yet." She pulled back until I reluctantly let her go. "Did you and Kerry have a fight?"

The drive up to Shropshire had given me a chance to think. Terrifying Tina was not on the agenda, neither was her thinking I'd lost my marbles.

"We're over, but she made me realise what's important."

"And that is?" Her hands were back on her hips as she peered up.

"You." I smiled at her defiant pose. "You're the most beautiful thing in my life."

Her jaw slackened as she searched for words.

"Uncle Ebb, Uncle Ebb, you're here." Tina's niece, Rosie, squealed, squeezing past to grab my hand. "Come see what Father Christmas..." The little girl giggled. "You got me."

"We need to talk," Tina mouthed as I was dragged

into the house.

* * *

Tina glared at me while I thoroughly examined Rosie's new Pie Face game. She was pacing by the time I distributed the chocolates and bottles of alcohol I'd procured from the newspaper offices. When her father suggested someone should check if his wife needed help, Tina leaped at the opportunity. She caught my arm and steered me towards the kitchen.

"Okay, buster, talk," she said, finally releasing me when we reached the back room.

The sound of music and clattering pans resonated from the kitchen we had just walked straight through.

"I love you," I said smiling warmly.

"I love you too, we've been friends for like forever." She frowned, confused.

"No, I love you." I moved closer, but Tina stepped back preventing me from gathering her into my arms. "I want you. I want our family. I want the Labrador. I want it all."

She put her hand on my forehead. "Are you sick? What have you done with my friend Ebb?"

"Tina, I want you." I caught her face between my palms.

"What?" Her eyes were wide open.

"I just hope you want me back," I said. "Let me kiss you, please."

"Are you high?" She put her hands on my chest and pushed firmly.

"High on love."

Her confusion was replaced by a serious look. "Ebb, we're friends. You're the best male friend I have. I don't want to ruin that."

I shook my head. "Then tell me what better foundation there is for a relationship than friendship?"

"Er... lust. You have to want to fuck each other," she said flatly.

I grinned. "There's no one I want to fuck more than you. Not just today but every day. I want us to grow old together. I don't want to ever lose you."

She looked doubtful.

"I want to show you how a lover should treat you. I want to tell you our son is old enough for a big-boy bike."

"What about what I want?" She furrowed her brow.

"I want to be the man you want. Please, give me a chance." I lightly ran a finger down her cheek. "Let me show you."

The door behind me closed with a soft thud. Probably her mother giving us some privacy.

Tina leaned back looking shocked.

"I'll show you." I smiled and stroked my thumb over her lips.

She briefly nuzzled against my touch before turning away and rubbing her face with both hands.

I waited. I'd had the whole night - and some crazy time travel - to realise what was important. Tina had gone from I'd killed Kerry, to I'm crazy, to me putting our ten-year friendship in jeopardy. I could wait a few more minutes to let her catch up.

Finally, she looked back at me though she kept some distance by resting on the wall behind her.

"Ground rules," she said, raising an eyebrow.

"Whatever you want." I nodded enthusiastically.

"I'm still waiting for for this to be a bad joke, but if we do this and it's weird can we just pretend it never happened and go back to being friends?"

"Yes. Yes." I leaned down to kiss her, but her hand blocked my path.

Damn, I loved this woman. There was the feistiness I'd begged her to show her waste-of-space partners, but with me it came naturally.

"You want us to be a thing?"

"Yes." I caught her wrist and drew her hand down, leaning in to kiss her.

"It's weird already," she said, just before I made contact.

"Let's just try. Trust me." My confidence was buoyed knowing this was the rightest thing I'd ever done in my life. "Kiss me."

"You do know this isn't a fairy story? I'm not sleeping beauty awaiting the kiss of my prince."

I caught her waist and tipped her backward with a flourish. "Sweet princess, please kiss this frog and make me whole again."

She laughed.

My fingers wound into her hair and massaged her scalp lightly. I gently rested my lips against her. She continued laughing. My other hand pressed into the small of her back, pulling her into my padded Santa stomach.

Gradually she softened in my hold. I traced my tongue lightly around her mouth and tasted her, and she tasted good. She relaxed more and let me slip between her lips. Cautiously her tongue met mine and moved slowly.

It felt right.

I couldn't believe how much time I'd wasted. All these years and the woman who made me happy had been right in front of my nose. I clutched her tighter.

Despite my comical attire, it was so natural, I was coming home. Tina was my home. I deepened the kiss and she moaned back. I let my hand rest on the back of her neck and circled my fingers.

Her breathing deepened as she stroked my fleece-clad arms. My body was alive with desire. Her touch was magical, the kiss igniting.

Tina's brother, David, cleared his throat and coughed behind us, making me jump and break the kiss.

"Sorry to disturb you two lovebirds, but we're waiting to eat and I'm hungry," he said with a knowing wink. "And I'd rather not get a free floor show of you corrupting my sister."

Tina blushed and hid her face in her hands.

"Mum's going to expect a big announcement after his dramatic entrance and you two running off for a quicky before lunch." David continued grinning at his beetroot-colored sister.

I put my arm around Tina and pulled her against my side. "I'm in love with your sister, and I'll happily announce it to the world."

"We're eating without you," Tina's dad bellowed from the dining room.

"Do you want to change?" Tina patted my padded stomach.

"Oh, shit..." I looked between her and her brother.

"What?" they asked in unison.

"I left my clothes in the office!"

The siblings dissolved into laughter and together, still laughing, we joined the rest of the family.

* * *

The dining room table had been extended out and a mismatched collection of chairs and stools meant we could all fit. Crackers and streamers covered the snowflake tablecloth.

I took the stool next to Tina and found her hand under the table.

"Wine or beer?" David asked, distracting me.

"Er... nothing, I've got to drive back," I said, letting go of Tina's hand.

"What? You're not staying?" her mum interjected while carrying in a large tray of roast potatoes.

"Yes, he's coming to Marley's with me." Tina's hand grazed my leg and found mine. With a squeeze, our fingers wound together. "He's just embarrassed he forgot his overnight bag."

"John, can you find Ebb some clothes? I'm sure we've got a spare toothbrush." Her mum put the tray down and headed back into the kitchen for more goodies.

"Marley?" I mouthed at Tina, feeling the hairs on the back of my neck stand up and it wasn't from her leg rubbing against mine.

"His place hasn't sold yet. Rosie has my old bedroom so I said I'd stay at his," she said quietly before smiling nervously. "It's only a five minute walk... unless you don't want to stay."

Looking at her beautiful face there was nowhere I'd rather be staying. I grinned at her before looking up at David. "In that case, the Sauvignon Blanc I brought is meant to be particularly nice."

* * *

Having recently seen this Christmas I can categorically tell you being part of the festivities is a thousand times better than just watching others' happiness. Throughout dinner, I touched Tina's leg and held her hand under the table, not that it stopped me eating so much food I probably didn't need the costume padding to look like Santa. After the food had been cleared away I relished being covered in cream during Pie Face. Everyone cheered when I kissed Tina's nose just as the cream was about to drop off.

The top half of my costume came off when we played Charades. Rosie thought I was hilarious in a white t-shirt, braces, and giant Santa trousers and boots. I was good and didn't cheat by shouting the answers I already knew.

Well-fed and a little drunk, I pulled on the Santa jacket for warmth and headed into the night with Tina. She was right; it took less than five minutes to walk down the street to Marley's old bungalow.

I swallowed hard as she unlocked the front door. The alcohol I'd consumed made me a little braver than my sober side would have been entering the lion's den.

She put the lights on to reveal an almost bare hallway. All personal effects had been stripped away and a solitary side table stood in the empty space. Good, the idea of Marley's things haunting the house was not fun. I just really hoped he wasn't haunting here either.

"Coffee?" Tina looked at me, embarrassed as she stood awkwardly in the hallway.

"Yeah, sure," I mumbled while scanning the walls for any poltergeists.

Satisfied nothing was about to attack I followed her into the small kitchen. It was also notably empty except for a kettle and tabletop fridge; even the cooker had been removed. The place was eerily silent.

Despite the wonderful day I'd had, the memory of my terrifying night was still fresh. I rubbed my jaw nervously.

Tina retrieved two mugs off the draining board and pressed the button on top of a radio, the only item on the window ledge.

"All I want for Christmas is you," warbled into the room.

The image of my parents, the staff party, and the little girl kissing her daddy through the computer danced in front of my vision. Warmth, peace and love resonated in my gut.

"Ebb, you okay?" Tina startled me.

I dropped my hand and shook my head slowly then smiled. "I'm not just okay, I'm fantastic."

I caught her waist and drew her into a slow sensual kiss. She froze but didn't pull away. I took that as a positive sign as I stroked my fingers against her shoulders. I sensed more than felt the barely perceptible change. Her mouth pressed a little more against me and her breathing slowed. I moved my lips to caress hers and she responded cautiously. My tongue slid just inside and with a sigh, she moulded her body to mine - as best, she could around the large Santa outfit.

She put down the jar of coffee and put her hands on my arms as she deepened the kiss. I buried my hands under the reindeer sweater and teased up her back.

She shivered and murmured into the kiss, before leaning back enough to speak.

"If this is weird we go back to just friends." She looked flushed.

"The weird thing is why have we not done this before?" I rested my palm on her cheek. "But I promise you, you're not getting rid of me. If you don't want me as a lover I will still always be by your side. You are my best friend and I love you."

She grinned, her eyes glinting. "Okay, Casanova, let's see what moves you've got."

I drew her into another passionate kiss, only coming up for breath to ask where the bedroom was.

Now I'd like to be able to tell you we smoothly made it into the bedroom and ripped our clothes off before making mad, passionate love. But you try getting out of a full Santa costume quickly. Tina, fully clothed, was sitting on the bed crying with laughter by the time I managed to disengage the top half. She appeared to lose the ability to breathe when I fell over trying to get the trousers and giant fluffy boots off.

Making such a fool of myself in front of any woman I was about to bed would've horrified the old me. Suave, sophisticated and smooth is the image I portray to the opposite sex. All except Tina, with her I felt comfortable to be myself, no pretence. I laughed with her until tears sprung from my eyes.

"Is there such a thing as comedy sex?" she asked when I collapsed breathless and naked on the bed next to her.

"You're about to find out."

I pulled her into another kiss. She continued to laugh as she kissed me back. I rolled her on top of me and let my hands wander under her sweater, teasing her sides lightly, making her shudder. I slid a finger under the cup of her bra and traced the underside of her soft breasts. She kissed me deeper, the laughter stopping and turning into a moan.

I left her breasts and reached around her to expertly flick the clasp of the bra open.

"Fancy moves." She smiled, sitting up and smoothly lifting the sweater over her head and letting the bra slip down her arms until she could throw the clothes on the floor. "This isn't as bad as I thought it would be."

"I can see your boobies."

"Ebb!" She slapped my chest then rolled her hips. "Well, I'm sitting on your cock."

"With far too many clothes on." My hands found the button on her jeans.

Let me tell you, getting jeans off a beautiful woman, sitting on my hard manhood, is not easy. But I'm a determined man, with some rolling and tugging I finally had her in just panties and blue and white snowman socks.

I leisurely explored her body, kissing along her collar bone then turning my face into the crook of her neck to nuzzle her. Inhaling her scent was intoxicating. Her fingers found my hair and she arched her back towards me.

Kissing my way slowly, I moved down and lavished attention on her breasts. Real, soft, perfect breasts. She had sensitive nipples and panted and moaned as my tongue curled around them. When I sucked hard she squealed and shuddered, pushing up to greet me.

Her hand moved down my side and tried to find my throbbing cock, trapped between our bodies as I lay over her.

I pinched one nipple and lifted my face off her glorious breast. "No, babe, just relax and enjoy this."

She gulped and lifted her hands to rest on either side

of her hair, fanned out on the pillow. Seeing her response I stayed on her breasts for a long time. I was in no rush; I knew we had the rest of our lives together.

Her fists balled with the effort not to move when I finally continued downwards and kissed each rib.

"Fuck, are you going to make me beg?" she gasped when my tongue teased around her belly button.

My fingers replaced my tongue as I grinned up at her. "You never have to beg. I'd give you the moon and stars if you wanted them."

She laughed loudly. "Who would've known you're such an old romantic."

"An old romantic with a carnal knowledge of a woman's body," I smirked and traced a finger over her panties.

"Shit," she squealed, thrusting her hips up, legs parted.

I pressed my finger a little more firmly, pushing the panties into her wet slit. Her legs spread more as I ran my finger slowly up and down the moist gully. She rocked and panted.

Catching one ankle then her other I put them on my shoulders and dipped my chin so my tongue could run over the panties. I tasted her through the flimsy cloth and damn, did she taste good. She gasped. Either side of the panties her lower lips were plump and red. They looked delicious. I sucked one making her throw her arms over her head and arch her back.

"Fuck, Ebb, fuck me," she sobbed.

"Always so impatient," I chuckled against her.

She lifted her legs and grasped them behind the knee. Wide and begging for more. I moved my attention to her other labium. Nibbling and kissing slowly up and back down.

She squirmed and moaned.

Resting on one elbow, between her legs I used my free hand to slip the panties to one side. The mixture of my saliva and her wetness shimmered in the low light of the bedroom. It looked divine. I dipped my tongue to suck some of the juices off.

Tina bucked towards me, but I pulled back a little.

She whimpered.

I blew a cool breath over her pussy. Thank you, Kerry-ghost, for that little trick.

"Oh my God, please," she wailed.

"Praying already, are we?" I propped myself up a little more so I could grin at her.

She bit her lower lip, staring back, wide-eyed.

I traced a finger along the crease of her leg. "Is it still weird?"

"Please," she sobbed, squirming under my touch.

I let my finger stroke just inside her folds.

She arched her back and gasped.

"What do you want?" My finger continued teasing her lower lips.

She sobbed incoherently.

"Tina, tell me what you want."

She sucked in several short noisy breaths before managing, "You. I want you."

That was what I had been waiting to hear. Painfully slowly I slipped the tip of my finger inside her pussy. Her walls clamped down as if trying to suck me in. She pushed her hips upwards and I laughed moving with her, not allowing her to take my finger deeper.

"Fucking bastard, please," she growled making me laugh louder.

I pushed my finger in a little more then slipped it out before using two fingers to slowly pump inside her soaking pussy.

"Yes. Yes. Fuck, you're incredible," she panted.

Keeping my fingers sliding in and out I moved onto my knees beside her. She was flushed, glorious and naked spread out on the bed. I'd never seen anything so beautiful. Her walls pulsed around me.

Never breaking the rhythm I turned my hand and easily found her engorged G-spot. When I pressed my fingers against it she wailed.

I rested my other hand on the slight swell of her belly to control her now violently undulating hips.

"You ready to see how much I want you?"

She garbled some sort of response.

I smirked, increasing speed and pressure.

"Fuuuuck!" she screamed.

I pushed her stomach firmly as my fingers pumped faster.

"Stop!"

I immediately froze but kept my fingers inside her throbbing pussy.

"I need to pee." Her hand flew to her mouth. "I'm so sorry."

I smiled and keeping my hand still, I leaned over to kiss her lightly. "Have you never squirted?"

"Huh? That's not a real thing." She pulled her hand away to look at me confused.

"Do you trust me?"

She nodded slowly.

"I want you to close your eyes and relax." I moved my fingers slowly inside her. "Can you do that for me? Let me show you."

She nodded again and her eyes fluttered shut.

"Nothing you do is wrong. Let go for me." I put my hand back on her stomach.

"I trust you," she said quietly.

"That's why we're going to work. You trust me and I'm going to live every day proving you're right." I didn't wait for a reply as I started working my hand faster.

The spongy flesh swelled and she writhed and sobbed. Harder, faster, hooking and pumping.

She screamed and went rigid.

I caught my breath, watching her, feeling her, hearing her.

A second later she erupted and fluid gushed out. She clawed at the bedspread. Her body spasming as a massive orgasm ripped through her.

I carried her through it until she was limp, sucking in noisy breaths as her pussy fluttered around my fingers. I slowed and eventually pulled them out. This is what Marley meant. My chest swelled with pride. Making a woman I loved collapse into a puddle of bliss was the greatest thing I could do and better than searching for my own ecstasy. This is what happiness felt like.

I lay down beside Tina and held her in my arms as she slowly came back to earth. I'd never felt so content in my whole life.

We spent the night thoroughly exploring each other. Our bodies and souls blended seemlessly and the sex was incredible. The ease we moved in harmony and the laughter made it magical. Experiencing the joy of a true connection made me mentally declare a total-abstinence approach to all other women, and I planned to never have intercourse with a ghost again.

* * *

That was the first night of many. We had both found our soulmate. Tina moved into mine full time once we returned to London. She was still hesitant about my long-term plans for our future, but the pandemic had an unexpected consequence. The first lockdown made her realize what was important, what Marley and his three stooges had already shown me.

Now we were both home working, we put in an offer on a nice house near her parents. This Christmas we'll be making a big announcement as she'll be twelve weeks pregnant. We would've got married over the summer if it hadn't been for Covid, but I think her mum will understand our reasons for delaying tying the knot.

I can't wait to meet my daughter. Tina doesn't believe me when I tell her I know our baby will be a girl, but she's happy to call her Hope if my prediction is right - which of course we all know it is.

The Ghost of Christmas Present was good for his word and spread joy and happiness. I wasn't the only person to gain from being in his presence. I did a relatively easy social media search and discovered he gave Bella and her husband their dream. They are now the proud parents of a tiny four-week-old baby boy, called Tim.

Thank you for giving me your time to hear my story. Tina and I wish you a peaceful and loving Christmas, and may I remind you, don't forget to share the happiness. Because if you don't Marley is still out there... and this year he might visit you.

Liam

Chapter One

"I'm not looking forward to the holidays, if I were being honest right now," my college friend Liam Jansen said from across the table. "It just doesn't feel right celebrating without Dad this year. On top of everything, my relatives are coming to town in the next few days probably after my money."

"This has got to be so hard to deal with right now, Liam," I said.

Liam's father, Liam Jansen Sr., had passed away a few weeks ago leaving his ten-million-dollar fortune to his only child, Liam, Jr. They'd had a complex relationship as the elder Liam wanted Liam to take over the family tailor-made suit business but Liam, Jr. refused to tell his dad he wanted to run his own cigar chain. Despite his father's objections, Liam actually made the right choice, became nearly as rich as his father which made him proud.

Liam's shoulders, beefy from working out earlier, were slumped over as he leaned on the table. Yet, he was as good looking as ever, so tall and muscular. His spirit wasn't broken, but it was definitely cracked.

"Thanks for dinner, Liam. This was amazing, as always. I'm happy to eat anyone else's cooking these days. Hey, just a thought, do you want me to help you get that timeshare ready? Thanks to Covid, I'm free."

"You would, really? It's just a bunch of cleaning and decorating, no fun at all."

"I haven't been anywhere in forever, nature seems to be the safest place possible. I'd be happy to help. Anywhere besides going from my house to Whole Foods and back."

"That's way too nice of you, Carrie but—"

"Another pair of hands won't hurt. If Ralphie tags along, I will be nicer."

"I think you like Ralphie more than me."

"Hmm."

"With all the lockdowns and shit, it really sucks that I had to lay off my father's employees."

"Yeah, that sucks," I said.

"Oh, I've got more shit to spill."

"What's up now?"

"Since this, all started, I haven't gotten laid. I'm scared as heck," Liam said drowning his second glass of wine for the evening.

"Oh jeez! Sounds like genital problems."

"It's weird but you know I can always be open about everything with you."

"Believe me, I remember your rendezvous like they were yesterday. Sounds like you need a long sex-cation..."

Liam chuckled. "I'll take that for one thousand."

"Have you been on Tinder?

"I've tried it but only old women show up on my matches."

Carrie shook her head. "This year's been hard for everyone."

"Christ, I've never watched so much TV in all my life."

"Same here... I've been binging Prison Break and Breakin' Bad reruns since February."

"I'm on my third go-around of NCIS so don't feel bad."

* * *

Liam finished showing me around his latest manufactured home and Ralphie followed us at every turn. I couldn't help but watch his sexy ass move as I walked behind him. I'd always been attracted to him but never wondered if we were compatible. The girls he went out with in school always wore loads of makeup and drank until they ended up in his bed till morning. He'd call me in the morning, still in bed with them asleep, telling how crazy his nights were. Now, he's a lonely millionaire while little ole me still trying to figure out life.

Then, came Covid 19...

Chapter Two

I wanted to check up on Liam since we hadn't talked for a while. I called him and thankfully, he had invited me over for dinner. I'd been way too busy trying to make a living, my life barely holding together. Working a sixty-hour-a-week job was the only way I could pay off my student loans, rent, and other shit.

Here's how I met Liam:

We did an internship together on a production tour in our third year of college, sweaty and grimy from hauling stuff and prepping. Amongst the crazy egos and extremely long days, Liam stood out the most dependable worker. Together with our colleague Aaron, we'd had some fun lunches and dinners together, and that had made all the difference on the grueling tour. And afterward, since we (Liam and I) only lived about thirty minutes apart, we'd met occasionally, finding we had in common a love for good music and TV shows. I felt like I could be honest with him about everything.

But deep inside, I had always wanted him. Since the first day I saw him on site with all that fresh ink over his body. At first I was scared of him -- this huge inked guy who didn't talk much. But once I was around him for five minutes, I knew he was like me, down-to-earth and real.

I noticed one day that several of Liam's tattoos weren't completed. I'd asked about this, and each one had a story like his friend had been dating the tattoo artist but then they broke up because his friend was cheating but he was just waiting for the woman to settle down and not express her anger at her ex by messing up his tattoo, so it might be awhile. I'd joked that he was probably the most patient person I'd ever met -- that even the unfinished ink on his body hadn't bothered him a bit and he didn't give a damn.

I was feeling tired and it would be a long drive home, so I told Liam I'd be heading out.

"I have an idea," I said after relishing his warm hug goodbye. "You can forget that I ever said this, but please don't get mad at me."

"I won't get mad," he said. I believed him. I'd never seen him mad.

"You know I haven't dated in years, Liam..."

"It's not the easiest thing, believe me, I know."

"What if, maybe, we added to our friendship..."

Liam looked puzzled.

"Just think about it. It could be good for us both. I miss having hands on me. It's been so long I can barely remember what the feeling is. Next weekend, we could just see if you feel like it. I think it could help both of us cope with this Covid madness. We're already been quarantined enough."

"You're right about that. Okay, I'll let you know," Liam said grinning. "You surprise me sometimes, Carrie."

"Just think about it. If you don't want me to come up next weekend, just text me."

"I'll text you anyway."

I patted Ralphie and waved as I walked to my car.

* * *

Oh my God! Liam replied back. I really didn't think he would. It hadn't been my sexiest proposal and I held my breath as I opened the text:

"I'll take you up on the offer. Get ready early Friday so we can head up together."

Wow, this is going to be fun.

"Works for me," I texted back. "Just text me the address and I'll meet you up there."

"Let me send you a driver..." Liam texted.

"No, I'll drive myself."

"Cool, I'll text you the address in a minute."

Chapter Three

I was definitely a ball of nerves on the ride up. It'd been a long, long time since I had—. *Let's just say I hoped I could be as patient and relaxed as I needed to be.* My body was already yearning for Liam, I told myself to calm down and stop pulsating. It was no hope, my panties were soaking wet. I pulled over a few times to adjust them and nearly masturbated at one truck stop.

It was a four-hour drive and it felt like an old friend. I remembered where to exit the freeway and which turns to make on the curving, hilly roads as I approached Mackinac Island. Liam Sr.'s timeshare was about twenty miles outside the city, close enough to head in for dinner in non-Covid times but far enough to feel rural. The up-north culture of endless boating and golfing in the summer, skiing and snowmobiling in the winter, and hiking anytime was all around us.

I arrived at an old but well-kept lodge surrounded by nothing but woods. Its trees creaked peacefully as they swayed from the wind. A thin blanket of snow had fallen, just enough to be pretty but not enough to challenge driving. Liam had already started a fire, and I could smell the woodsmoke as I got out of the car. He'd heard me drive up, and Ralphie rushed at me through the door, barking. He jumped on my legs and tried licking my face, and I petted her.

"How was your drive?" Liam asked, walking up. "Let me get your bags."

"If you insist," I said, handing him the larger one. "I've always loved the drive up here when I was younger."

Ralphie followed us inside, after jumping and dancing in the snow.

"This place is huge and gorgeous."

"My dad saved all his life for it. I'm glad he got to enjoy it. I may have to sell it, but we are having one last Christmas here first. Let me show you around."

We walked through the open kitchen to the living room. A massive stone fireplace dominated the space, the blazing fire casting light and shadows all over the room. Leather sofas, live-edge log tables, wool blankets, amber-glowing lamps, and iron accents completed the log-home décor.

I turned to Liam and looked into his eyes.

"How are you doing?"

"I'm okay. I'm glad you made it."

I gave him a hug. "I'm glad, too. Whatever way helps, I'm here for you."

"I'll put your stuff in your suite."

"Suite, Wow! Ok, Mr. Liam, What's first: the Christmas tree or—?"

"Dinner," Liam said. "Are you hungry? I made some homestyle chicken stew."

"Oh yeah, let's eat."

* * *

Liam told me a little more about the place his father cherished so much as we ate.

After supper, Liam went over to the sofa and patted the seat next to him. I came, and Liam leaned in, kissed me, cautiously at first. For the first time in a long time, I felt sparks.

Liam pulled back, and I smiled as he pulled me onto his chest. I laid back, my arms around him and his around me.

"Carrie, this room's going to need a tree. Not sure if we should use a real or fake one?"

"I won't be here to water it all week. So fake it is."

"Don't be like that, Carrie. Good things come to those who wait."

"Okay—I'm just playing. I feel sleepy, babe; the food and wine are kicking in. Let's get up.'"

"Ok."

I got up, Liam grabbed my hand and took me to the basement.

Fifteen minutes later

We brought up the tree and decorations from the basement closet. I swept the floor and then dusted the log wall while Liam put the tree together. I plugged it in and was ready for the next step.

"Carrie, you can't turn the tree on until it's all said and done," Liam said. "Family rule, been that way since I was a boy."

I shook my head.

"Well, my rule is that we need the best Christmas music for this."

"And a drink," Liam added. "Feel like some champagne? There is an old bottle that I remember seeing downstairs."

"Sure."

* * *

The music played in the background on the Apple TV, and the tonight's mood had officially begun. Liam handed me a glass of champagne as I looked into the box of ornaments.

"What do you guys do, ribbon, tinsel, the whole nine?"

"Just ornaments and lights. We're simple folk."

"I can handle that."

I parsed through and picked out the most ostentatious ornaments. It would be easier to balance those out first, and then add the demure ones. I got started, moved around and concentrated.

Liam left for a few minutes, bringing logs from next door. The fireplace was shared with the master bedroom, and I guessed that he was starting a fire in there, too.

Liam settled onto the sofa when he was done. I glanced over, and he was watching me.

"You could help, you know." I said teasingly.

He was quiet for a moment, gazing at me and the fire. "*Baby, it's cold outside*" filled the room. The fire crackled and blazed an amber glow on us.

Chapter Four

"I have a dare for you. Every time I look at the tree, I wish I had a sexy topless Mrs. Santa next to it."

I chuckled, taking another sip of champagne. I was already feeling it.

"Hmm, okay. You have to undress me."

"Come over here."

I paced slowly across the room.

"But those big windows," I said, "Someone is going to see me..."

"Are you afraid a deer might see you? There's no one for miles."

"It's cold over here."

"Let me add some logs to the fire."

Liam took my hand and pulled me in closer as he stood up. He kissed my lips, and then unbuttoned my blouse, working his way down. Moments later, it was off of my shoulders and down my arms. Instantly, my blouse fell to the floor, as I stood in my black bra.

Within seconds, Liam reached behind and unclasped it, pulling it off.

"That's it," Liam said, smiling. "This will be my 2020 tree-decorating screenshot."

I strolled back to the tree as Liam added a few logs to the fire.

"This is ridiculous. Am I going to be your pinup, Mr. Santa?" I asked.

"Not from where I'm sitting," Liam said, sitting back and sipping his champagne.

"Finish decorating the tree."

"Are these orders, Mr. Claus?"

"Yes, Mrs. Claus."

I finished hanging the ornaments and then reached way up for the star. I looked over, and Liam was still watching my every move.

"Now do I get to turn it on?" I said. "Does it pass your inspection, sir?"

"Everything passes," Liam said, looking from my breasts into my eyes.

I found the button and turned on the tree. Then I turned off each of the lights in the room. There was only the glow of the fire and the colored lights on the tree.

"The tree is reflecting off you. Little spots all over your chest. You have to let me take a picture."

"Oh my God, Liam! I don't know."

"I won't get your face only that sexy body of yours."

"Okay."

Liam got up and moved closer, framing my breasts in his phone. *I couldn't believe I was allowing this.*

"I want to get a shot of you back, too."

Liam spun me around, moving my hips and framing my back angled against the tree's lights.

Then he put his phone down and next his hands were on me. My breasts were against his chest as I looked up into his eyes.

"I can't believe you're here. I've wanted this for so long."

"So have I."

"Merry Christmas!"

"Merry Christmas to you, too, sweetheart!"

* * *

Liam kissed me, his fingers traced the edge of my boob. Then he grasped it, the pressure against my nipple made me moan.

Liam then pulled me down onto the sofa, and I laid back on the pillows. He suckled me from one side to the next, and I moaned.

"Oh Liam," I groaned as he pleased me.

He went on for a long time, and I laid back and enjoyed, my arms above my head grasping the sofa.

"As big as your tits are, I've still not got much going on," he said.

"This is the best I've had in years."

"I think we should get in the family hot tub."

"Um, only you would put one in the middle of nowhere."

"You're right about that."

"Am I the first girl that will get to test it out?"

"Honestly—yes."

"Good," I said after I kissed him.

"Before you came, I turned it on. It should be nice and hot by now."

"Well, it being winter and all, I didn't pack a bathing suit."

"You're more than welcome to wear nothing."

"Not just yet buddy," I said, giving him a kiss on the cheek as I got up. "I'll be right back."

"Take your time, sweetheart."

* * *

I went into my room, and pulled off my jeans and panties and slid on my PINK shorts I brought for my little home workout. I tucked my hair in a ponytail and came back out.

The door was already open to the deck, and the hot

tub was right around the corner. Liam was already inside, and my cup of champagne was already refilled.

Liam gazed at me as I walked over, the cold, snowy deck boards under my feet made me move quickly. I hopped into the tub, the swirling water a welcome change from the biting chill.

"Oh this is nice," I said, reaching for my glass. I took a sip and set it down.

The stars were so bright, and snow on the ground reflected the moonlight.

"This is so wonderful, Liam. Thank you for inviting me here."

"Thank you."

I floated closer to him, and he pulled me in for a kiss. I gripped the side of the tub for stability. Then, he drew me in, and I held his shoulders, sitting next to him and leaning in.

"Can I touch you?" I asked.

"Of course."

I trailed my hand down, over the hair on his chest and rested it on his tummy. Then, slid my fingers down and gripped his cock, still mostly not erect. *I could change that within seconds.* I reached for his scrotum, taking his balls into my grip. I looked into his eyes as I did this.

"Are you okay?" I whispered.

"Just fine," Liam said, laying his head back against the

rim of the hot tub. He moved his arm around my shoulders and pulled me to his side.

I played with him under the water for a while, then I straddled him.

He smiled, as he gripped my ass. My breasts were closer to the surface now, sometimes becoming exposed when I moved.

I kissed him deeply, bracing myself on the edge of the hot tub. His hands wandered, trailing down from my back to my ass, sliding under my PINK shorts.

"Take these off."

I slid them off and put them on the deck.

I moved back onto Liam's lap. He kissed me, his cock was rising. His hands moved back to my ass, and then he used my thighs to pull me closer. Our privates made contact, and I gasped. I inhaled and relaxed myself into him. It felt amazing to be in full contact, our bodies melding into one.

Under the stars, in the warm swirling water, being with this billionaire friend of mine, I'd wanted for so long.

"I'm really enjoying this," I whispered.

"So am I."

His hands were on my ass again, one slipped in between us.

"Sit on the edge. I want to see you," I said.

Liam pulled himself up and perched on the rim of the hot tub. I opened his legs, looking at his long, half-erected cock for the first time. My body was still submerged except for my head.

"Are you okay?" I said, looking up.

Liam nodded.

I sucked gently, feeling Liam getting harder by the second. Simultaneously, I began sucking his balls, jerking his shaft up and down.

Liam was so big—the largest cock I'd seen in person, in fact. *This was going to be an interesting night.*

I dove my mouth back onto him, gagged, and took in as much as I could. "My God, Liam. You've been blessed..."

"Oh, Carrie, Oh Carrie," he kept moaning.

I felt Liam was about to come and I think he knew it. Suddenly, his hand now was on my shoulder when he started shaking.

"Let's get in bed," he said rushingly getting up.

"Oh my God! You were about to ..."

"I know," he said chuckling.

* * *

Liam got out first and handed me a towel. He then quickly pulled the cover onto the hot tub as I ran inside.

I toweled off for a minute before diving under the covers, not wanting to lose the heat from the water. Liam joined me a few seconds later, crawling under with me.

"You're wonderful, I can't believe we waited so long for this."

I answered by kissing him. He shifted on top of me, covering me with his body. I felt my wetness rise, I was getting ready for him. His hardness was on me, driving me crazy. I put my arms around his back, pulling him to me. His chest hair tickled against my breasts as he moved down, suckling each one in turn. Then Liam reached down, finding me quite slick for him.

"Are you ready?" he whispered.

"Fuck me but be gentle -- you're really big, Liam."

I moved my knees apart, and Liam put the head of his cock into my folds slowly, watching my reaction. I moaned as it inched in, my walls squeezing tightly around it.

Then, Liam pumped slowly. I moaned gripping his shoulders.

"Are you okay my love?"

"Yes, don't stop."

He thrust more, bracing on his arms. I was lost in the little explosions in every molecule of my body. Liam increased his speed, and I clutched his ass, telling him in go faster.

"Oh, Carrie, Oh Carrie, I'm coming..."

Liam exploded all inside me, grunting, and seconds later, became still above me. I opened my eyes and his were closed. I held his face as he continued to coat my walls until he was finally emptied.

"I haven't felt this good ever," I said smiling.

"Me neither."

Chapter Five

The sun was beaming through the clear windows as I opened my eyes. I felt Liam shift as I peeked over.

"I have to tell you something, Carrie. You're my first redhead."

"Well, you're my first guy with ink."

"What do you want for breakfast?"

"Anything. I'll be in the shower while you cook."

"No clothes when you come out. Just a robe."

"Fine. But we're going to have to work at some point, my dear, if you want to be ready for your family..."

"We're getting there."

I kissed Liam and got up to go shower.

* * *

The hot water reminded me of what we'd done in the night. I was so proud of myself. *No more masturbating in the shower or at least for now!*

When I came out of the bathroom, the aroma of breakfast filled the air.

"Come here," Liam yelled, standing at the stove in his boxers. His ass looked so sexy. I came and he put his arms around my waist as we watched the eggs fry.

"Scrambled eggs are the best. Thank you."

"You're welcome," Liam said, moving my wet hair to the side and kissing my neck.

"You're feeling better then," I said.

"Package delivered."

"Where's my baby Ralphie?"

"Outside for a run. He loves the snow."

The sun shone brightly through the wall of windows, turning the eating space into a greenhouse. I sat down to orange juice and a fruit basket.

"This is already the best I've had in awhile," I said.

Liam brought over our food and we started eating.

"So what's the plan for today?" I asked.

"Well, hanging garland, stocking the fridge, prepping the bedrooms with fresh sheets and towels, hanging lights outside. And other stuff."

"Dirty boy," I chuckled. "Where do we start?"

"From the bottom up," Liam said, gesturing downward. "You must have me under a spell or something. Ready to go again?"

Liam reached over and opened my robe and I didn't deny him. "It's your turn."

We removed the dishes and Liam slipped his hand inside my robe, reaching my shoulders, and made it fell to the ground. His bare chest was against mine, and the sun warmed us, skin against skin. His hands came between us, massaging my breasts as I slid mine into his boxers, feeling his hard shaft.

Liam guided me back toward the table, and then onto it. Then he leaned in, gazing between my legs which were spread open.

His tongue explored my labia. Then it went deeper, making me moan his name. I caressed his hair as he worked. He hit my g-spot and I came hard, arching up and crying out.

"Oh my God! Fuck Liam. I'm coming already."

"I want to remember this moment," he said. "I enjoyed every bit of your sweetness."

I scooted my hips down to the edge of the table. Liam stood between my legs, dropping his boxers. I reached for his cock, and he put it in me. My body, of course, welcomed him in. Liam sighed closing his eyes, his body lost in my wetness.

He pumped vigorously, finding a rhythm that

matched his urgency. My breasts moved with each stroke. I wanted to grab him underneath, but instead I remained still and concentrated on the feeling.

His hands gripped my hips. I panted, feeling another orgasm coming. He speared faster, and I came audibly as he came with me.

"You're trying to get me pregnant, Liam?"

"You're on the pill, right?"

"Don't ever ask a lady that after you came inside her. It's rude, Liam."

"Sorry my lady." Liam pulled a blanket over us and I settled into his warmth.

"Switching topics... I didn't expect that we'd have such great chemistry," Liam said.

"Well..." I got up, still pissed off at him and walked over to the table. I bent over slowly and grabbed my bathrobe then I tossed his boxers somewhere.

"Was that a fuck-me right on the table for Christmas dinner pose?" Liam said.

"I hadn't actually thought of it, but yes, that works."

I put on my robe, and he kept staring at me.

"I suppose I should get started today. Before you get me off track again," I said.

"At this point, I couldn't care less about fucking Santa Clause, trust me."

"Liam, go get groceries. My pussy can't take that sword stabbing me no more this morning," I pouted.

"I thought it felt good," Liam said.

"Seriously, I'll hang the garlands and prep the rooms. You go and hurry. I'll take care of Ralphie."

"You're the best, babe."

Chapter Six

Minutes later, I began working. Cleaning and decorating someone else's home was a lot more fun than my own.

Another blanket of snow overnight, and with the sun shining on it, made the roads sort of slippery. It would take Liam a while to get to the city and back. Ralphie followed me from room to room before getting bored and heading to her corner for a nap.

I was glad for the break. Going from having no sex for years to lots over the last twenty-four hours was mind-bending. It was electric so much so that Liam's peck on my cheek before he left, could still be felt.

I'd need to keep it together though. I was certainly the type to get attached.

Liam was single but for how long? Was I the type he wanted a relationship with? That was on him to decide.

And in his state of grieving, there was no way I'd rush him.

* * *

I struggled through the frustrating parts of my workday; getting the garland hung and lit, dusting, vacuuming, and decorating every room. Once there were fresh sheets on each bed and towels in each bathroom, I took a moment to look around. *Not bad for only a morning's worth of work.*

I was dusting the hearth when Liam walked in, big bags of groceries in his arms.

"Want some help?" I asked.

"No, you've done plenty today. I've got this."

"Fine, if you don't want me, I'll be right over here," I said.

"Oh, I wouldn't say that."

I blushed, turning back to what I was doing.

Liam came up from behind me and kissed me on the neck. "I missed you so much."

"Me too, sweetheart."

Liam brought some pasties and we sat at the family table.

"I can't believe you got so much done while I was gone."

"Well, that's the power of a woman." I chuckled. "Much more satisfying than cleaning my own. Now, everything's ready for your crazy family."

"Thank you, Carrie. I really appreciate it."

"No problem."

"Hey, want to walk over to the neighbors' with me? The old guy never answers his phone, I need him to drop off a load of firewood this week."

"Sure as long as you don't share me!"

"Oh my God, Carrie, you are so naughty!"

"I suppose so."

* * *

On the way back, Liam was getting closer to me. The trail was narrow, and I'd taken the lead, able to follow our footprints from before.

"I have to tell you, just you walking in front of me is turning me on," he said. "I'm going to have a big problem this weekend."

I looked back at him. "Happy to activate, my friend."

Liam did look like he was walking a little funny. Something popped up into my head as I saw his cock rising out of his jeans. I glanced around -- no houses or people in sight.

"Come here," I said, taking his hand and then pushing him against a tree.

I kissed him as my hands found the waistband of his jeans, then I unbuttoned them, unzipped and slid my hand in, jerking his already hard cock. He kissed me, groaning in my ear.

"Oh, Carrie! You're so bad."

"I know, Liam."

I then got on my knees, ignoring the snow. Into my mouth fully, my lips eagerly engulfed him. Liam leaned back and gasped. I looked up as I sucked the tip, flicking my tongue against the underside. His eyes were closed as he gripped my head.

Liam's balls were now in my mouth, I gently sucked them. He moved his feet apart, bracing more against the tree.

Moments later, I again sucked his large cock like a young girl enjoying her lollipop. It was so long and beautiful, it forced me to focus. Only after a minute or so, I felt Liam twitch, and he came all in my mouth. I swallowed every last drop and held steady, so the cold air wouldn't be a shock when I released.

When I looked up, he was still braced with his eyes closed, lost in his climax. I stood up stiffly, my wet knees reminding me of what a crazy choice this had been. I smiled as I gently slid his cock back into his jeans and buttoned him up. He took me in his arms, looking into my eyes.

"That was amazing, Carrie. Thank you again."

"That's what friends are for."

"Holy shit. I can't believe you did that out here."

"As you said earlier, who is the deer going to tell. And maybe now the squirrels," I said laughing.

Liam laughed with me.

"I like watching you come. It excites me to know that I have you at my disposal," I whispered.

"Hmm, that's a good feeling to have," Liam said. "Let's get you home before your knees get too cold."

* * *

Liam took my hand and led me down the path. Before long, the house was in view, the sunshine reflecting off of the metal roof and the Christmas tree was shining through the windows.

"I need to hang the lights before dark. Go warm up by the fire. Turn on some Christmas movies or something."

"I can come help," I said.

"No, you've done plenty today. Go relax."

"Ok, baby." I kissed Liam and entered the house first.

Chapter Seven

I changed, came back out front, and made tea. Liam had brought back Christmas cookies from town that would go perfect. I added some more logs to the fire, and then I did find a Christmas movie to watch; *Kiss Kiss Bang Bang*.

A dirty weekend couldn't but help the mood. Everything was heavenly; the bells, decorations, firewood, Liam, and this great place.

I got lost in the movie and barely heard Liam come inside.

"Are you watching Kiss Kiss Bang Bang? I did not think you were the type, Carrie." Liam chuckled

"I can't help it, I got sucked in the moment." I smiled. "Wanna watch something else? Did you finish with the lights?"

"Almost, but it's getting dark and I need a break."

* * *

I slipped on my boots and walked outside to see Liam's setup. He followed, and so did Ralphie, bolting into the snow.

"Looks festive," I said, seeing the lights along the roofline and wrapped around the timber columns. Wreaths were hanging from each porch section and a few lighted figurines.

"Your family will like this."

"They are an ungrateful bunch who will barely notice, but I know my late dad would."

I started to shiver and Liam put his arms around me.

"I think he would. He'd be so proud of you, Liam."

We walked back inside the house only after a minute of being outside. It was too cold.

* * *

The evening was simple and cozy. We were in our pajamas including Ralphie and had dinner by the fire, watching Christmas classics and drinking hot toddies. I relished cuddling on Liam's chest as the snow started to fall heavy outside.

After the second movie, sleep was starting to overtake me. It had been a long day.

I sat up and Liam knew I was ready for bed.

"Do you want me to sleep in your room tonight?"

"Of course, I want you too."

"I need to shower first. See you soon," I kissed Liam on the cheek and stood up.

* * *

I was taking a shower and before I finished, I caught Liam peeking through the steamed-over shower door.

"Can I join you?"

I smiled, and Liam came inside. He put his arms around me from behind, held me by my waist and kissed my neck.

"You look so hot right now."

The water ran over Liam's tatted muscular body. "You look pretty hot yourself, big boy."

Liam went straight for my breasts, fondling them gently. My nipples puffed and I caught myself feeling dizzy from the steam.

"Liam, let me meet you in bed, okay?"

"Okay, baby."

I got out and toweled off.

Once I hopped in bed, I saw Ralphie had taken her place by the foot of the bed. I turned off the lights, but before so, I checked to make sure my chemise and light makeup were perfect.

* * *

I must have dozed off. I woke to the feeling of Liam stirring behind me as I laid on my side nuzzling my neck.

"You're so patient," I said. "I'm sorry I fell asleep."

"You've earned every right to sleep," Liam said, trailing his hand up my thigh, "I'm open to other ideas." His fingers touched my labia.

Liam's hard cock was right on my ass and now his hand slipped over my breast, gripping the nipple.

"Oh, I'm awake now, honey," I said. "Oooh, Liam! Don't stop..."

Chapter Eight

We made love for a very long time. It felt like episodes of a clumsy middle-of-the-night sexcapade; a sleepy mix of trying out different positions while we grasped for each other in the darkness. Liam took me from behind first, spearing into me as I cried out his name. And then I rode him to a climax, he yelled my name as we came together. I clenched him and unloaded thrice on his lovestick. Then, I stilled above him, riding the feeling for as long as I could.

"You're beautiful," Liam said.

I slid off and lounged next to him on my tummy. I was more awake now that I'd come.

Liam caressed my backside, moving down my spine to my ass.

"How many times have I come this weekend?"

Liam giggled. "I was going to say the same."

“So, in joking fashion. Do you think your dad would approve of us using his house for this?”

Liam put his hand over his mouth.

"Carrie, you’re so naughty but I have to tell you something...”

“What Liam? I’m sorry if I was—“

“No, Carrie, you’re okay. I wanted to say that I don't want this to end.”

"Okay, is that all you want?” I was hoping Liam was going to be serious but who knows. “I’m willing to see where this goes. I’m being serious.”

“I am, too, Carrie. I mean it. And not just because of this," he said, rubbing my mound. I have to admit I got a little booty for a white girl but hey!

* * *

We slept until the sun was high. A couple more inches of snow had fallen, Liam got up and shoveled snow from the porches and walks and hanged the rest of the Christmas lights.

"Done," I said when he came back in. "Now all you need are presents, people, drama..."

Liam chuckled.

"Is the hot tub still on?"

"It is."

"Do we have time for a quick soak before I head back home?"

"I'll make time."

* * *

I put on a bathrobe and shedded it as I climbed in beside him, all need for modesty gone. My nipples puffed right away in the chilly air as the forest surrounded us. The white winter blanket made the warm water feel even cozier.

I snuggled into Liam's arm, slowly warming up in the heated water.

"I'm really glad I invited myself up here." I smiled, settled onto Liam's shoulder.

"You've turned a Christmas I was dreading into one that I will never forget," Liam said. "And I'll be counting the days to New Years."

"Cheers to that!" We clicked our glasses then kissed.

Tanya

Chapter One

"All right, everyone. I've got some bad news. So listen up."

Tanya Jackson sat in the dining room of the Camden Food Bank. The full-time secretary of the nonprofit, she sat with the other staff members and twenty regular volunteers, waiting for the director to speak.

It was a late Monday evening, two weeks before Thanksgiving and her heart was heavy because though she already knew what he was going to say, it didn't make the blow hurt any less.

The director of the CFB, Brother Nicholas Finley, known in the community as Brother Nick, took a deep breath before continuing, a sad look on his face.

"Now, everyone, you all know that donations have been down this year," he said. "The pandemic has really taken its toll on our donors. We're finding that the people and companies who used to donate to us, are now either in need of donations themselves or just don't have the extra funds to send to us. As a result, our cash and food donations are now down over fifty percent."

Tanya held her breath, knowing what was coming next.

"Therefore, if our donations aren't up in the next two weeks," he continued, "We'll have to shut down indefinitely. Which means we'll be shutting down before Thanksgiving, our busiest time of the year."

A chorus of gasps and groans went up through the small crowd. The Camden Food Bank had been a saving grace for the past twenty something years. Located in South Jersey, they were responsible for providing food to six neighboring counties, which housed over sixty food pantries, emergency shelters, childcare centers, soup kitchens, senior centers and night shelters that directly served Camden's homeless, unemployed and working poor.

Tanya enjoyed working at the food bank, especially on Thanksgiving and Christmas Day. It warmed her heart to be able to help, but this year their circumstances were dire. Her deep brown eyes teared up as she continued to listen to Brother Nick.

"I do have a few ideas up my sleeve," Brother Nick said, smiling. "For example, Joshua, the assistant director, and I will be doing several newspaper and TV interviews to promote our cause. And here in the office, Deb and Tanya are going to keep making phone calls to local businesses to see if they can donate more."

Tanya nodded over at Deb Ross, the treasurer of the CFB. For the past month, they'd been calling local companies to secure additional donations, but they weren't making much headway.

"Anyway," Brother Nick continued, "I just wanted to let you know what's going on. And to ask you for your help. We really need a miracle this year, so I'm counting on all of you to help us stay open."

Brother Nick spoke a few moments longer, then adjourned the meeting. Tanya gathered her belongings, put on her coat to protect herself against the chill, and headed out to her car. But before she could reach the door, Brother Nick stopped her.

Standing a full six-feet-four inches to her five-feet even, he towered over her. However, his warm smile always put her at ease. He placed his hand on her shoulder. "Tanya? If you can, come in early tomorrow morning and get started on those donor calls. Every little bit will help."

"Sure, Brother Nick. I'll come in an hour early. I'll be in at about eight."

"Thanks, Tanya. And I know that you'll be blessed for your help."

Tanya frowned as she pulled her coat tighter, a sudden chill ran through her that had nothing to do with the weather. What Brother Nick didn't know is that she was single and lonely. Men weren't on her list nowadays but a desirable woman was if she had her head screwed on right.

"I think we could all use a miracle this holiday season," Tanya muttered and walked out the door.

Chapter Two

First thing in the morning, Tanya opened up the office, then went to the kitchen to put on a pot of coffee. The men in the warehouse opened at nine, so Tanya had a bit of peace and quiet before the other employees came in.

Since it was so early, no clients were due in yet, but there were still mounds of paperwork to finish, in addition to the calls that she and Deb had to make.

When the coffee was done, she went to grab a mug out of the cabinet and happened to glance out of the window at the far end of the kitchen. As she saw her reflection, she studied herself.

Tanya adored her rich, cocoa-brown skin and curvy features. Her smile was bright and her hair looked great in her voluminous curls. Also, Tanya's heart was as big as they came.

However, Tanya felt that her twenty-nine years of age were slowly catching up with her. "When did I get old," she wondered as she studied the tiny wrinkles near her eyes and her thickening figure. "It seemed like I was just in college yesterday, and five years later look at me.

"I just wish I were able to go to Grad school," Tanya said sadly.

Sighing, she walked over to her desk and got to work.

* * *

By the time Deb came in an hour later, Tanya had gotten through the first page of businesses, but with dismal results. By their lunch break, neither of them had had much luck. They received plenty of '*No, not this year's,' a handful of 'maybe's' and only one or two 'yes's'*.

After lunch, as Tanya picked up the phone again, she looked toward the ceiling. "God, we really need a miracle," she supplicated softly. "And I really need one, too," she added.

Next business on Tanya's list was the Kroger's in Cherry Hill, New Jersey. She dialed, then waited. A young female answered and Tanya asked for the manager. When he came on the phone, Tanya introduced herself and launched into her speech about donations they needed for Thanksgiving.

The manager, Rick, was helpful. He recommitted their prior support of the CFB but there was one problem.

"Well, we'd love to help you with some donations, Ms. Jackson," he said, "But this holiday season, Kroger has instituted a new practice: All donation requests must now be processed through our corporate office first. If you can hold, I'll get you the number."

Though Tanya was a bit put off by the extra hurdles they'd now have to overcome, she was hopeful. "Okay, Mr. Gonzalez. I appreciate you."

* * *

"All right. The name of Kroger's National Director for Corporate Giving is Ms. Christine Lewis. She's in New York City. Would you like for me to transfer you to her office?"

"Sure, and thank you."

As Tanya waited, a shiver ran through her. "Goodness! I used to know a *Christine Lewis*. In fact, I had a huge crush on her back at Rutgers" Then she laughed, embarrassed, "I mean, what are the odds it's her?"

Then a woman's voice came on the line. "Hi, this is Christine Lewis for Kroger Corporate Giving. How may I help you today?"

Oh my God, Tanya thought. *That soft, yet husky voice? It couldn't be...*

"Hello???"

Tanya stuttered. "Um...I'm sorry. Hello. I'm Tanya calling from Camden, New Jersey." Then, she paused vexed.

"Yes? Hello?"

Ugh! Get it together, Tanya.

"Hello. Oh, I'm sorry. I'm Tanya calling from Camden, New Jersey and I wanted to find out about your donation programs. Our local food bank would like to apply for assistance. I was switched over to you by Rick Gonzalez, the manager at Cherry Hill."

"Sure. Just let me get some information first. Okay, what is the name of your organization?"

"The Camden Food Bank."

"And the address and phone number?"

Tanya gave Christine the information.

"And tell me a little bit about your program, please?"

Tanya told Christine about all the great work they did in the community. That they had been actively supplying over fifty food pantries and shelters for just over twenty years, and how this year due to the pandemic, their program was in dire need of additional support.

"Well, I need you to fax me the following; your program's brochure, a formal request letter from your director on official letterhead, your tax information and 501(c)3 certification letter. Can you do all that for me?"

"Sure, sure I can. Please give me your fax number."

Christine gave her the number. "Oh yes," she added. "What's your name and number? I need a contact name for my paperwork."

"Um...my name is Tanya Jackson."

There was a short pause.

"Tanya Jackson?" Christine asked.

Then there was another pause.

"Tanya, your voice sounds so familiar! Did you happen to go to Rutgers? About, say, ten years ago? Like around 2009-2010? And were you in the Black Student Union?

Tanya's heart nearly beat out of her chest. "Ycs. Yes, I did," Tanya answered.

"Tanya! This is me, Christine! Christine from the RU! Don't you remember me?"

Tanya played it off. "Oh, Christine! Of course, I remember you! I wasn't sure it was you. How are you doing?"

"I'm fine! And I'm just sorry we lost touch after all those years ago. It's so good to talk to you!"

Tanya nearly blushed. "It's really good talking to you, too."

"Now, normally I don't do this," Christine said, "But why don't I make a trip down there to check out your food bank in person? Do you think we could we work that out?"

"Sure."

"Okay, I have some vacation time, and I need to use it before the end of the year. Since there's only a couple of weeks before Thanksgiving, why don't I come this week?"

"Okay."

Then there was a slight pause, and Tanya thought she heard pages rustling.

"Okay," Christine said. "Today's Tuesday. Why don't I come down there Friday morning and stay the weekend? How's that sound?"

Tanya was dumbfounded. "Sure," she repeated.

"Well, it's a date, then!"

Tanya shivered at the word '*date,*' but was determined to keep it together for the sake of the CFB. "Thanks, Christine. I really appreciate it."

"Now, unfortunately, I can't promise anything because I have to get the okay from my boss first, but I'm going to do everything I can to help."

"I understand," Tanya said.

"So I have your number here and I'll call you Thursday afternoon to confirm.

"Sure," Tanya said for nearly the tenth time. "That sounds great."

They spoke for a minute longer, exchanged good-byes, then hung up. Afterward, Tanya sat at her desk, quiet for a long time. *That was Christine Lewis,* she mused. *That tight slim body she had, oh my! I wonder if she's got a man,* Tanya thought.

Moments later, she dismissed the thoughts from her head, and went back to the next company name on her list.

* * *

That night, as soon as Tanya got home, she took a steaming-hot shower, put on a satin nightshirt, then went to fix herself some hot cocoa. Taking the mug into the living room, she plopped on the couch in front of the TV.

Thoughts began swirling in her head once more causing her to unable to concentrate on the screen. She clicked the TV off, laid back and reminisced about Christine.

They'd met freshman year at Rutgers and through their work in the BSU or otherwise known as the Black Student Union, they sponsored on-campus seminars, charitable events, high school outreach programs and other events that celebrated Black history.

Throughout the year, though Tanya dated a couple of guys, but was more interested in girls, and had been for a long time. With the stigma of being less accepted in society, Tanya kept her sexual preferences on the down-low.

Yet, Christine was always her number one crush; straight and lesbo.

Christine was cute and sexy. She was one of the most attractive girls on campus and always had a love for the Black community and humanity in general.

"I wonder how she's doing," "She must have somebody," Tanya mused. "She's probably married with two kids."

Tanya looked around her empty house, a two-bedroom brick home on Wildwood Avenue. Her mom and younger brother lived in Philly, less than five miles away; however, she still desired a warm, caring closeness with someone she knew at least. Unfortunately, the holidays were quickly closing in, and Tanya had no prospects to speak of.

"Maybe next year," she sighed and settled in for the night.

Chapter Three

"You have a very nice facility here," Christine said after Tanya showed her around CFB's compound.

That Friday morning, Tanya had picked her up from the airport and, at Christine's insistence, instead of taking her to her hotel room, had taken her right to the food bank. Tanya had given Christine a tour of their facilities, then introduced her to a number of their staff and volunteers to give her a better picture of their work on the ground.

"It looks like you're doing a good thing here," Christine said.

"Yeah," Tanya said as she led Christine back into her office. "We're trying, but we have so much demand, and not enough supply. It's the kind of job that can be very rewarding, but very depressing at the same time."

Christine nodded. "I can certainly see that. At Kroger, we try to do all we can, in as many communities as we can, but more and more people need help. Now more than ever because of this Covid 19."

Tanya went to her desk. "I know you got my fax, but I wanted to give you some hard copies of our documents," Tanya said as she handed Christine a folder. "It's got all the info you requested: the brochure, the letter from our director, our tax info and our 501(c)3 certification."

"Thanks," Christine said as she flipped through the papers. She then slid the folder into her briefcase. "Now, I still have to run this past my boss, but I gave him my preliminary report right after you called, along with some news articles I pulled from the Internet. It's looking good, but I won't have official word for a few more days."

"That's fine," Tanya said. "Anyway, I appreciate your help."

"Anytime," Christine smiled.

"Well," Tanya said, checking her watch, "It's almost time for lunch. Wanna grab a bite to eat? I'd have to get back to work pretty soon, but we can at least have something quick together?"

"Sure," Christine said. "And after lunch, you can come back to work, after you drop me off at my hotel. Now that I've seen your facility, I can work on sending another report to my boss before the workday ends."

"Well, you don't have to stay at a hotel. I have plenty of space at my place. And I have WiFi so you can email your boss." Tanya stopped speaking and held her breath.

Christine hesitated then smiled. "Hey what the heck! I can say the company a few dollars!"

Chapter Four

"So how've you been?"

Tanya smiled at Christine as they sat. They both chose chicken salads for lunch along with some hot cocoa.

Before Tanya answered Christine's question, she took her in.

Christine had the same smooth, luminous, warm caramel skin tone like it was when she had been in college. She was still tall, lean and still had that nice little mini-curly afro. Also, she still looked analytical as ever with those nerdy glasses on.

"I've been doing okay," Tanya answered. "But what about you? What have you been doing all these years?"

"Well, just after graduation, I got married."

Tanya winced. *There goes that fantasy*, she thought.

"Wow! That's great," she said, with as much glee as she could muster.

"Don't be. We've been divorced for a little over two years now."

"Are you all right now?" Tanya asked.

Christine sighed. "I never should have gotten married."

"To him?"

"No, to a guy in general."

Tanya's eyes widened. "Really? That means...you're—?"

"I guess I always knew, but I never really wanted to deal with it. But now? I'm cool with it. My family still hasn't come around, though," she said, taking another sip of hot cocoa. "And it's been over two years now, but what can I do? I have to live my life, right?"

"Right. Well, when I first came out, my mom—"

Christine's head snapped up. "Excuse me?"

"I said, when I first came out, just after high school, my mom had a problem with it. But later on, she admitted that she always knew. In fact, she was kind of waiting on me to tell her. Now, she's okay with it." Then Tanya stared at Christine for a moment. "You know, there's a good chance that your family will come around, too."

"Yeah. I know."

They sat there for a few moments, each lost in their own thoughts.

Christine sipped on, then began to speak. "Tanya, there's something I need to ask you. Why did you transfer schools? It wasn't until we came back for senior year that I even knew you were gone. What happened?"

Tanya sighed. She hadn't told this story to anyone.

"It was my mom," Tanya began. "She got sick just after Christmas break that year. She wasn't eating, was nauseous all the time, and just run down. She went to some doctors and had a lot of tests, and just before the school year ended, we found out that she had leukemia."

"Oh my God," Christine said. "That's horrible!"

Tanya nodded. "She's doing well now, but back then? Our family barely had the money to send me to school, let alone to cover mom's doctor bills. We didn't have any health insurance, so we were pretty much on our own. I dropped out of school and came back here to finish two years later so I could take care of her and to work full time."

Tanya took another sip. "In fact, things got so bad, that we had to use a soup kitchen ourselves. Thankfully, there was one right near our house."

"Hmmm...That's why you're so dedicated to the food bank," Christine said. "That's pretty admirable."

"Yep. We came to the Camden's Community Soup Kitchen almost every night. And we went to the Baker House Food Pantry for groceries once a month. So, yes, I'm committed to helping the people that helped us. Eventually, I got a job with CFB after graduating and I've been there ever since."

"You know," Christine said, "I did Google your name over the years. It's just that 'Tanya Jackson' is a pretty common name. Very common. Plus, I had no idea where you lived. I didn't know that you were in Camden." Christine looked off in the distance. "I thought that you moved to Atlanta or something."

Tanya blushed. "Girl, wait. You searched for me?"

"Yeah, I did," Christine said, looking back at her. "You were my girl in school. It hurt me when you didn't come back. It's sad to know that things had gotten so tough for you, but I'm glad to have finally found you again."

"Really?"

"Yup."

Tanya was silent as her mind began to spin. *Could she really be interested?*

Just then, Christine looked at her watch. "It's almost one now. You have to get back soon?"

Tanya glanced at hers. "Yeah. Let me go drop you off at my house first. Just make yourself at home and I'll be there around fiveish."

Christine smiled as they stood and gathered their belongings. "Thanks, Tee. Gotta get this report to my boss or he'll kill me. Who knows maybe I'll have something special for you for later after I finish."

A thrill went through Tanya as they went to the cashier. "Hmmm...sounds good! I'll take you up on that!"

* * *

Once Tanya got home from work, she was pleased to find that Christine had made dinner for the two of them. Though it was simple, Tanya was on Cloud Nine at Christine's thoughtfulness.

They talked late into the night, reminiscing more about school and how their lives had changed over the years. They then exchanged stories about their jobs, finding several similarities, in that each loved to help their communities.

Also, both learned that the other was single, but nary a move was made.

* * *

They spent the following morning, taking a drive around Camden and its surrounding communities, where Tanya showed Christine more shelters, and centers like CFB. Afterward, they took a long lunch in neighboring Philadelphia. Tanya raved to Christine about Geno's Steaks on the way and Christine for the first time, had one.

Tanya was the perfect hostess, making sure that Christine's every need was taken care of. But often, when she thought Christine wasn't looking, she stared at her, and was overwhelmed at the feelings she was having for this woman.

Tanya wanted to massage Christine's shoulders, kiss her on the neck and play in her hair but since she was staying in the guest room on the other end of her house, she seemed so far away.

Unfortunately, neither made a move.

* * *

Early Sunday afternoon

Tanya reluctantly drove Christine back to the airport.

"I had a wonderful weekend," Christine said as she pulled her luggage out of Tanya's trunk. They were standing at the curb in front of the terminal with Tanya's car still running. "It was so good to see you."

Then Christine's mood seemed to dampen. "I'm going to miss you, you know."

"Now you know we don't have much time here," Tanya joked, trying to lightened the mood. "The parking police are such a bitch. They like giving tickets here."

"Then I'd better make this quick."

Christine leaned in and hugged Tanya, then kissed

her in the mouth. "I'm so glad you're back in my life. I'll talk to you soon, boo."

Christine waived as she grabbed her bags and headed into the terminal.

Tanya stood there for a moment, stunned. Then she touched her lips and smiled.

Chapter Five

Monday morning, Tanya kept that huge smile as she opened the office. She put on a pot of coffee and readied her desk for the morning's work. She had many more calls to make, but her weekend with Christine left her giddy and unfocused.

Just then the phone rang. She checked the clock. At just after eight, the office wasn't open yet, but she went ahead and answered, anyway.

"Camden Food Bank, this is Tanya. How can I help you?"

"Hi, Tanya. This is Maureen Langley at Bank of America."

Tanya was elated. Camden's Bank of America was their largest donor. Though they hadn't yet submitted their yearly holiday donation check yet, Tanya was sure that Maureen would send it over right away.

"Hi, Maureen. What can I do for you?"

Maureen paused. "Tanya? I have some bad news..."

Tanya listened in horror as Maureen explained that they weren't going to make their donation this year.

"We'd really love to help, Tanya," Maureen explained, "But as what usually happens when cuts are necessary during a crisis, the first to go are the charities, unfortunately."

Maureen and Tanya spoke a few minutes more, then they hung up. Dazed, Tanya first thought about calling Brother Nick, but then decided to wait until he came in before she gave him the bad news.

"What a way to start a week," Tanya thought, as all memories of Christine faded away.

Chapter Six

Tanya sat in the food bank's dining area, in a meeting eerily similar to the one they'd had two weeks prior. It was now the Monday before Thanksgiving and Brother Nick had called a special meeting.

Things were looking dim since all the week before, like Bank of America, a great number of their largest donors were either substantially decreasing, or canceling altogether, their donations.

Brother Nick had been sullen for several days, with an important decision to make: whether or not to close the Camden Food Bank until further notice.

Tanya had been fielding calls all the week before from food pantries, shelters and centers, but she was just as clueless as anyone else as to what Brother Nick would do.

As she watched, Brother Nick slowly took the podium in front of the staff and volunteers.

Just as he was about to speak, one of the volunteers, Connie, came out of the kitchen and into the dining area. She motioned to Tanya. When Tanya walked over to her, Connie whispered.

"I know you said to hold all your calls until after Brother Nick's meeting, but this one is urgent."

Tanya frowned as she followed Connie back into the kitchen. "Who the heck is it?"

Corinne watched as Tanya picked up the extension on the wall. "She says her name is Christine. Christine Lewis."

Tanya's heart fluttered as she answered. "Hello?"

"Hello, Tanya? It's me, Christine."

Tanya's eyes glanced at the floor. "Hey, there. It's good to hear from you, but I'm going to have to call you back. We're actually in a meeting. Our donations have not only not gone up, but they've dried up since we last spoke. I think that Brother Nick might be about to cancel the program for the holidays."

"No! Don't do it!" Christine said. "Tell him not to cancel!"

"Why not?"

"I have a surprise for you. For all of you. But I'm not quite sure of all the details. So just stand pat. On

Wednesday, everything will work out fine. I promise! Go tell him not to cancel the program! Go, go!"

Tanya said a quick goodbye, then ran back into the dining room.

Chapter Seven

Wednesday morning, Tanya arrived to the office fifteen minutes late. For some reason, just before she turned off the main road onto the road leading to the office, there was what appeared to be a log jam of vehicles blocking the exit. There were about ten Kroger trucks lined up back to back and Tanya cursed as she had to maneuver around them.

Still vexed for arriving late, Tanya put on a pot of coffee, and before she could get back to her desk, her phone rang.

"Hello?" she snapped. Then she caught herself. "Hi, Camden Food Bank. This is Tanya. How may I help you?"

"Hello, Tanya. This is Matthew McConnell. I need to know where to park."

"Excuse me?"

There was a pause. "Have you looked outside?" he asked.

Tanya put the phone down, went to the window and looked. She gasped at what she saw.

Out in the parking lot were the ten trucks, all in a line, back to front. Somehow, they had all moved from the main road to right in front of her office. All of the trucks were marked '*Kroger*.'

She put the phone back to her ear. "I'm sorry. What is all of this?"

"Ma'am, we have a delivery from Ms. Christine Lewis, Kroger Corporation and the WNBA."

"The WNBA? The Women's Basketball Association?"

Just then, line two rang. She put Matthew on hold and answered. "Hello?"

"Tanya! It's Christine. I'm at the front door. Can you let me in?"

Tanya dropped the phone and ran outside. She saw Christine on her cell phone standing next to the first truck. Its driver was leaning out of the window.

"Hey Tanya!" Christine called out. "This is Matthew. He needs to know where he can unload. In fact," she said, waving her hand at the other trucks, "They all do!"

"God is good!" Tanya exalted.

* * *

While they were outside, Brother Nick pulled up. Tanya and Christine ran over to him as he got out of his pickup. "What's going on here?" he asked.

Tanya pointed to Christine. "This is Ms. Lewis. Thank God, she's the one who brought us these donations."

"Donations?" Brother Nick asked. "What donations?"

"Those," Christine said as she pointed to the trucks. "I called in and got trucks filled with food and other groceries." Then Christine pulled out an envelope and handed it to Brother Nick. "And I also have this for CFB."

"My God! What's this?" Brother Nick asked.

"It's a check for one-hundred thousand dollars," Christine said. "And there's more where that came from. Much more."

"Thank you. God bless your heart, Ms. Lewis," he said as he hugged Christine hard, his eyes watering. "Thank you so much! Happy Holidays to you!"

"Happy Holidays, Brother Nick!" Christine then motioned back toward the trucks. "We need to know where to unload these babies. There's quite a few perishables in there, too."

"Right this way, my dear!"

Brother Nick went over to the drivers as Tanya and Christine stood out front. They watched as Brother Nick directed them to the warehouse in back.

As the convoy started to pull off, Tanya turned to Christine. "How did you do it?"

Christine chuckled. "First, my boss was so impressed at what you all are doing here, that he gave us permission to donate the food from our warehouses and our biggest vendors. About the cash, some of it came from my closest friends, but most of it came from the WNBA."

"The WNBA?" Tanya asked. "How?"

"I'm a season ticket holder with the New York Liberty. I knew that they had a corporate-donor relationship with Kroger. I just called the WNBA corporate offices and voila! We got paid! Also, as a special treat, some of the players and coaching staff are coming here tomorrow to help serve Thanksgiving Dinner."

Tanya was overcomed with joy. She pulled Christine into a big bear hug. "Thank you! Oh my God, Christine, I love you!"

Christine laughed. "You're welcome. Love you, too." Then she leaned in close to Tanya's ear. "Tonight, be ready for me, mama. I'll be over at eight," she said in a low, seductive tone.

Shivers ran through Tanya as her body began heating up. "Okay, boo. I'll be ready."

Christine then said, "Tanya, I'm looking forward to

being there with you more in the future. Our future. Would you like that?“

She hugged Christine even tighter and whispered in her ear.

“Oh yes, and I promise you, I’ll be a good girl!”

“You better or I’ll spank you.”

The couple chuckled as they embraced each other in all smiles.

The End

Dominic

Chapter One

Dominic came downstairs, looking for his wife, Bernadette and found her standing out on the balcony of their hotel room. Picking up his leather jacket over the railing, he went to the door and stepped outside.

"It's cold out here, honey," he said draping his jacket over his wife's shoulders, then wrapping his arms around her.

"I know honey," Bernadette said, leaning back against Dominic. "But it is so lovely out here. The view is amazing."

"Yes, it is," Dominic said, kissing Bernadette as they watched as the sunset painted the snow-capped peaks. "We have a few hours before Christmas. What should we do?"

"I'd love to go for a walk with my prince charming,"

Bernadette said, pointing down below to the back of the hotel where there was an ice-skating rink with a few couples hanging out.

"Your wish is my command, love," Dominic said, kissing Bernadette's cheek.

"Let's get dressed."

"Ok, sweetheart."

After a half-hour, the couple and their escort, Bill left the hotel onto the snow and followed the winding path finally ending up at the rink. They watched the skaters for a few minutes and then Dominic said, "Would a noblewoman of your grace like to go ice skating?"

"I'd love to with you, my prince."

Dominic lifted Bernadette's mitten to his lips. "I'll go and get the skates," he said, brushing kissing her hand.

"Hey Bill, do you skate?" Bernadette said to her long-time personal bodyguard. Bernadette was a celebrity fashion designer.

"I do. For four years on my high school's hockey team."

"Three pairs then. What sizes?" Dominic said.

"I already know. Ladies-Nine and for you, Bill?"

"A ten, Dominic. Thanks."

"No problem, bud.

Dominic headed to the rental booth and minutes later,

he and Bernadette were gliding hand in hand, melding in with the other skaters. Bill followed them, watchful of any suspicious activity.

Dominic spun his wife around, skating backward as he pulled her along. "Have you seen the women trying to get Bill to skate with them?"

"I have, poor Bill."

"I see they've stopped trying now. They must think he's gay," Dominic said and Bernadette giggled.

"Maybe, it's always the good-looking ones getting picked on."

* * *

They skated for about an hour and then left. They returned down the winding path until coming upon a lighted area where some clearing had been set up with wooden chairs and barrels. A fire was burning and people were sitting around it.

"Oh, Dominic, look it's a live nativity," Bernadette said, taking in the outdoor scene of a manger with live sheep and goats. "Can we stay for a bit?"

"Of course we can, my love." Dominic leaned down to kiss his wife's nose. There was a notice that the next show was in about ten minutes. The trio moved to find seats as close to the front as possible.

The lights lining the seating area went out, leaving

only one bright one directly above the manger. Some music came on and the performance began.

Dominic missed most of what was going on; he was too busy watching Bernadette. Her face was lit in childish wonder as a retelling of the special birth was played out.

When the performance came to an end and the light above the set went out, a hush fell over the crowd – the moment was a special one.

* * *

"Oh, that was beautiful," Bernadette kept saying as they made their way back to the hotel, her head leaning on Dominic's shoulder.

"Yes, it was," Dominic said.

"I'll tell our niece, Louisa. I know she would love it. It would be lovely to have something like that in our back yard, don't you think?"

"It would," Dominic said just as they reached the back of the hotel. "Before we go inside there is something I have to do. I promised Louisa. It was a part of this Christmas getaway she planned for us," Dominic said grinning.

"And what's that?" Bernadette said, turning.

"This." Dominic bent down and took some snow. Seeing what Dominic was about to do, Bernadette held up her hands.

"Don't you dare, Mr. Collins."

Dominic formed a snowball and slowly went to Bernadette. "Why not honey?" he said, tossing the snowball back and forth in his hands.

"Because... Dominic...," Bernadette said backing away.

"Well, you have to give me a reason," he said, lobbing the ball from hand to hand.

"Because I'll kill you."

Dominic stayed silent for a moment and then said, "I'll sacrifice my life over it." He threw the snowball, deliberately missing Bernadette.

"Bill? Help!" Bernadette said.

"Sorry, Ma'am. You're on your own. I'm staying out of this one."

"Coward," she said quickly diving to make a snowball.

Snowballs were sailing and the couple played until Bernadette said enough.

* * *

The telephone woke Dominic. He groaned as he rolled over Bernadette, to answer it.

"Hello."

"Merry Christmas, Uncle Dominic." It was Louisa. Dominic winced a little at the volume in her voice and said, "Merry Christmas, sweetheart." He got out of bed, the long cord on the phone followed him to the window. He began speaking softly not to wake Bernadette.

"Yes—yes—well. She's still sleeping... I'll have her call you when she gets up."

"I am up, Bill," Bernadette said. When Dominic turned around, she said, "Looks like I'm not the only one."

"Who's that?"

"Hey, sexy. Behave yourself," Dominic whispered as he brought the phone over. "Your niece might hear something." As Bernadette spoke to Louisa, Dominic put on some tight candy-cane boxers Bernadette got him the night before.

Bernadette put her hands over her mouth watching Dominic's crotch erect. She stuck out her tongue as Dominic walked to the bathroom. When he came out, Bernadette was still on the phone. Dominic then went downstairs to make some coffee.

* * *

Dominic was on the sofa, drinking and munching on fruitcake when Bernadette came down.

"I'm so sorry, darling," she said as she reached the bottom of the stairs. "You know Louisa. Our niece is a talker."

"I do," Dominic said. "I made you some tea."

"What time is it?"

"About six."

"Hmm, I knew there was a reason why I married you." Bernadette kissed Dominic and laid beside him.

"Santa's in town—" Dominic gestured downward.

"I see," she said picking up her teacup.

* * *

After they ate breakfast, Dominic put on a Santa hat. Bernadette giggled while passing out the gifts from under the tree. She waited to open hers until they were all piled on the coffee table; hers in front of her and Dominic's in front of him.

"Wishful thinking, Mr. Collins?" she said laughing as she opened the first gift – pulling out green silky cami, matching bra and g-string.

"Can't blame a man for trying," Dominic said chuckling as he opened his first gift; a watch.

"There's something written in the back," Bernadette said as she set the box of lingerie aside and picked up the next present from him. Dominic pulled the watch out and turned it over. "For all time," he read, "All my love, Bernadette."

"Wow, this is perfect, sweetheart," Dominic said drawing Bernadette's mouth to his to kiss. "Thank you, my love."

"You're welcome," she said unwrapping another gift in

her lap. She pulled the top off the square-shaped jeweler's box and gasped, "Oh, Dominic."

"I wanted you to have something to remember our time here."

"Oh, baby. It's gorgeous." Bernadette exhaled pulling the necklace out; at its end was a diamond-studded snowflake. She bent over and Dominic slipped it around her neck then gently kissed her forehead.

"I knew it was for you the moment I saw it."

Bernadette squeezed his hand as she turned to open several more. The last gift had a card attached to it reading: "You hold the key to my heart." She opened it and inside was another necklace but the pendant on this one was a key – made from white gold covered in sapphires and diamonds.

"Dominic, oh my God!"

"You like it, huh?"

"Hell yeah!" Bernadette kissed Dominic nonstop. "Thank you."

"You are welcome, my love."

* * *

One last gift, which was the largest, was hanging off the table for Dominic. He opened the card seeing his wife's hand in salutation.

"The music of my life began with you," It read.

Dominic looked surprised as he began removing the wrapping paper.

"All you talked about was getting another guitar," Bernadette said as Dominic pulled the guitar out of the box. "I found an artisan in town—he makes them by hand in his shop. I knew when I saw them, it would be the perfect gift."

Dominic put the guitar against the table and reached out, pulling Bernadette until she was in his arms. "Thank you, my love," he said before kissing her.

Bernadette tucked her head up licking his ear feeling the warmness of her husband's torso against her.

"Well, since you're already dressed for a performance, won't you do one for me?"

"My pleasure."

Dominic played some of Bruce Springsteen's hits next to the fireplace. Bernadette was curled up in one of the armchairs while Dominic sat in another playing for his wife long into the morning.

It was noon when they headed upstairs to shower. Friends and family texted Bernadette during Dominic's mini-guitar performance saying they would like to get together for Christmas dinner.

Chapter Two

"It's been a very long time since I've been pampered," Bernadette said to Amy as they left the spa, heading down towards the elevator.

"You should do this more often, girl. You deserve it."

"Maybe, I should. I have time now that Louisa's running my day-to-day stuff at Bene in town." Bernadette chuckles. "Life isn't quite as busy as it was when I was running things all by myself. I couldn't even think about having an hour to get my nails done even on a day off."

"I hear you, girl."

They were near the elevators when they passed the 'ladies room' sign.

"Hey, I'm supposed to meet Dominic at the fireplace," Bernadette said. "I don't want to head all the way upstairs to use the bathroom," she turned to her bodyguard standing behind them. "Mark, I'll be going inside."

"Yes, ma'am."

"I'm going back up and rest a bit before we have dinner," Amy said yawning.

"Of course, dear," Bernadette said. "You go on ahead I'll see you later."

"Alright." Amy headed to the elevators. Once she got on, Bernadette turned to Mark.

"Shall we," she said. Mark nodded and led the way. "Wait, while I check things out."

"Okie-dokie."

"Hello! Anyone inside?" Mark stepped in while Bernadette checked her phone.

"It's all clear, Ma'am. I'll be here"

"Thank you, Mark."

* * *

"You know that I let you win, right?" Mark's nephew, Anthony said as he and Dominic left the pool hall.

"Keep telling yourself that," Dominic said tapping the young man on the shoulder. "I beat you fair and square. Face it, boy...you suck."

"Come on, uncle. You don't have to rub it in." Anthony said. "I'll bet my aunt can beat you."

"Oh, she beats me in a lot of things but no pool." Dominic said, amused by the look on Anthony's face. He was just about to say something when out of the corner of his eye he saw Mark standing in front of ladies' room.

"Hey, Dominic," Mark said smiling.

"Hey, bud. Are the ladies inside?"

"Only Bernadette, sir. Amy went back up to the suite."

Dominic nodded and Mark stepped aside allowing Dominic to enter. As the door closed, he heard the lock click and Anthony put his hand over his mouth. "I'd wait in the lobby with little Anthony if I were you. You wouldn't want to hear anything that would compromise us."

"Yes, sir." Mark blushed and went with Anthony to the lobby.

* * *

Dominic leaned against the door inside and waited.

"Think being with me and leaving Uncle Don and Aunt Bernie alone is okay?" Anthony said.

"Yeah, son. Why would you say that?" Mark looked for a place to make sure they could be close but not too far.

"I guess you would say that." Anthony laughed. "Let's just say that when I get my uncle's age, I hope I'll have half the energy he does."

"You're making it seem like you and I are dead."

"Pretty much," Anthony said. "I'll leave the lovebirds

for you to watch. I'm going upstairs. See you tonight, Mark."

"Ok, bud."

* * *

Bernadette came out and was at the sink. Dominic smiled as he made sure the door was locked.

"Hello, stranger," she said, seeing her hubby in the mirror.

"Hello," Dominic said as he came closer. "How was your spa day?"

"Beautiful, thanks for asking."

Dominic came behind her and put his hands on her shoulder. He then kissed her shoulder.

"My lady, you smell good," Dominic growled as he nuzzled the curve of Bernadette's neck and shoulder.

"It's the cherry almond oil the masseuse put on me." Bernadette tilted her head to the side. "Maybe I should go more often."

"Definitely," Dominic growled as he grasped her chin and tilted her head back. His mouth captured hers.

Their tongues tangled battling for dominance – lunging and parrying, thrusting and retreating in an erotic imitation of the more intimate act they were craving.

As the kissing went on, Dominic's hand slid from Bernadette's chin down through the open neck of her blouse to grab her breast. Bernadette arched, pressing herself deeper into his grasp.

When she was about to turn around, Dominic pulled his lips from hers.

"Don't move," he panted against her cheek. Bernadette only nodded and Dominic's tongue darted swiftly back into her mouth.

"My love," he breathed pointing to the mirror and Bernadette lifted her gaze to meet his in the mirror watching his hands slowly unbuttoning her blouse. Dominic then pulled the fabric out of the waistband of her pants and parted the silky fabric. Pushing it back off Bernadette's shoulders, his hands skimmed up her torso to the front of her green lacy bra; his Christmas gift. Dominic unfastened the clasp and peeled the cups off. "My God!" he said as her breasts bounced satisfying his hungry gaze.

Bernadette moaned feeling Dominic playing with her breasts and teasing her nipples. "Dominic..." she breathed as her hands slid to grasp his ass pulling him in.

Dominic's cock poked her backside. "This makes you wet?" he said biting Bernadette's earlobe.

She replied by taking his hand, sliding it down to the button closure of her pants. Dominic popped the button, slid down the zipper and growled something when he saw the green g-string in the mirror. Grasping the edges, he eased them down her hips and gave a push until they slid down to her feet. Bernadette kicked them aside, craving his touch where she burned for the most and took his hand to guide it.

Bernadette gasped and shivered as Dominic's fingers glided over her mound finding the slickness of her desire. "My God! You're so wet—" His fingers then parted her. Her hips bucked the instant he touched her clit, rubbing it with his thumb. Dominic slid two fingers deep inside and massaged gently. Bernadette's moans grew as he stroked. The sweet torture went on until she could take it anymore.

"Dominic... god, Dominic please," Bernadette gasped as she dropped her hand to grab his wrist while he was still fingering. "I need your cock now, please big daddy...Oh my God—"

He obeyed kissing her as he fumbled for his belt, then the button and finally the zipper.

"Hurry—daddy before I—" Bernadette moaned, pulling her mouth from his as she reached to help him as he shoved his jeans and boxers down. "Lean forward." Bernadette, of course, complied. Widening and bracing her hands on the countertop, he put the head of his cock along her lips, coating himself with her pussy then positioned himself. With one thrust, Big Daddy entered.

"Fuck—Yes. Daddy..." Bernadette shouted.

Dominic began thrusting, bending forward stretching his body until he laid against her back, pressing his mouth to the back of her neck; his hot breath against her skin. Bernadette turned, seeking his and he captured her kiss;

his tongue moved in and out in rhythm to the slow pumping. One hand rested firmly against her chest, keeping her pressed to him and as he felt his ejaculation building along with Bernadette's. He took his free hand, stroking her clit as he rode.

"Oh god, Big D...Dominic... like that...yes... yes." Bernadette moaned as she rocked to his rhythm.

Dominic knew she was close to coming. He took her earlobe between his teeth, nibbled and growled. "Come for big daddy, come for big D—"

"D...Dominic..."

He felt her walls contracting around him. "Come, baby" he growled as he squeezed her clit. That was enough to send Bernadette over the edge. She screamed his name as she came, her walls clutching and pulling at him, relentlessly massaging his hardness as he picked up the pace of his stabbing, plunging harder and faster as he strove for his own.

"Ah.. oh god...my love..." Dominic groaned his orgasm was just out of reach. Bernadette pushed herself up so she could slide her hand down and grasped his nuts, giving it a squeeze. "Come for me now," she said gently rolling his balls in her hand.

"Ah, Bernadette..." Dominic growled as he came, spilling into her as his body spasmed. Dominic clung on, kissing as the waves of pleasure slowly ebbed.

"Oh god," he lifted Bernadette from her waist.

"You can say that again." Bernadette kissed Dominic's forehead. "I don't think we've ever made love in front of the mirror in a public bathroom before."

"There's a first time for everything."

"We should head up to the room before dinner," she said between kisses.

"I think you're right."

Once dressed, Dominic slipped his arm around Bernadette and led her to the door.

He turned the lock, opening the door and Dominic chuckled when he saw Mark waiting in the lobby, the poor guy was looking a little green around the gills.

"You okay there, Mark?" Bernadette said.

Dominic grinned as he took Bernadette's hand and tucked it inside his arm.

"Yes, sir," Mark said clearing his throat. He blushed as the couple approached.

"Great. Let's get ready for the evening," Dominic said and Mark led them toward the elevators.

Chapter Three

When the couples finished dinner and exchanged their goodbyes, Bernadette gasped when she saw what was parked in front of their vehicle.

"Dominic," she said. "What's in the world!"

"I thought my lovely wife would like a sleigh ride up the mountain to the Springs." A large sleigh pulled by a team of Clydesdales.

Dominic led Bernadette over to the sleigh.

"Good evening, sir, ma'am," The driver said, turning around in the rider's seat, holding red leather reins.

"Evening." Dominic smiled as he helped Bernadette up.

"You'll find a thermos of hot chocolate and a couple of mugs in the box underneath the seats. The wife makes the best hot chocolate in the town. I'm Jacob, by the way... but you can just call me Jay," the man said as he turned back to face the horses.

"Thank you. We're Dominic and Bernadette."

Dominic and Bernadette settled into their places taking a woolen blanket beside them and spreading it over their laps; tucking the ends in to keep out the chill.

"All settled back there?"

"Yes, thank you," Dominic said as he put his arm around Bernadette.

"Alright then," Jacob said flicking the reins of the horses. The bells on their harnesses jingled in the night air.

Bernadette laid on Dominic's shoulder and he kissed her forehead. "Happy, my love?"

"Blissfully," she said as she tucked her head inside.

"Good." Dominic kissed Bernadette underneath the blanket while holding her hand and enjoying the beauty of the ride up the mountain. Occasionally, the calm was interrupted by their driver giving them a bit of history and trivia about the area they were going through.

Thirty minutes later, the sleigh pulled up to the entrance of the outdoor pool and two-story bathhouse.

"Here you are. I hope you enjoyed the ride," Jacob said.

"It was lovely, thank you, Jacob," Bernadette said.

Dominic got out first and helped his wife down. "Do you wish me to stay for the return?" Jacob said.

"No, thank you. We'll be okay," Dominic said giving

Jacob a tip. "Thanks again for the ride and Happy Holidays."

"You do the same, sir."

* * *

The bodyguards followed the couple as they went up the steps to the bathhouse. As they approached, the door opened. Once inside, a receptionist greeted them.

"Welcome to the Cascade Upper Hot Springs. I'm the director of the Springs. As per the request of your security team, the Springs has been closed to everyone. I'll be in my office over there if you need anything. Please enjoy."

"Thank you." Bernadette smiled.

Their head guard for the evening, Mark turned to Dominic. "I'll keep two guards here at the door. The rest of us will patrol the building. According to the blueprint, there are no other entrances to the Springs except by climbing up the fence which has cameras everywhere," he said. "But if you want I can have my men outside to keep watch."

"No, I think what you have in place will be just fine," Dominic said.

"Great." Mark smiled watching as Dominic took Bernadette's arm and walked with her toward the changing area. They left each other; Dominic to the men's change room and Bernadette to the ladies.

The couple dressed up in robes given to them by the resort's staff along with flip-flops. When they got to the door of the pool, Bernadette began shivering. Dominic hugged her as they made their way to the pool. Bernadette dipped her foot in.

"Ooh..."

"Too hot?"

"Oh no," Bernadette said as she untied her robe, dropping on the tile. As the cold air hit her skin she shivered and then quickly got in the water, sinking below until only her head was above water. "Oh it's lovely, baby," she sighed as the heat from the water pierced her body. Bernadette swam until she reached the center. When she came up, she brushed her hair back and turned to Dominic who still stood at the ledge. "Care to join me, Big Daddy?"

"Is that a name you just said one day you'll pick out for me, Miss?"

"Maybe," Bernadette said winking. "Why don't you come in here and find out."

"Well, I'm not one to pass up a challenge, especially one that involves steam and water." Dominic grinned taking off his robe. He dived in, swimming over to Bernadette. Once he reached, he pulled her in closer. "Now, what were you saying?"

Bernadette leaned and pressed her lips to his. It was a brief and light kiss and then she slipped from his arms.

"Now you have to catch me," she said diving underneath and swimming away. Dominic laughed and swam after her.

They played a game of chase and keep away for a few minutes until Bernadette let Dominic catch her. He grabbed her ankle and pulled her back. She came up and Dominic pulled her right into his arms. "See, Big Daddy knows how to catch his fish."

"Mmm, I see you do," Bernadette said as she put her arms around him. "Now that you've caught me, what are you going to do?"

"Oh! I'm sure I'll think of something," he said running his fingers dancing up and down the curve of her back.

"Oooh! I'm sure you will," she said shivering to his touch.

"Wrap your legs around me," Dominic said helping her. While hugging, he carried Bernadette over to the end of the pool to the area of the steps. He set her down until she was seated halfway out of the water. When Dominic would have kneeled, Bernadette said, "Lay back. I have a better idea."

Bernadette moved close to the hot length of Dominic's cock while Dominic's hands were on her back holding her in position. The water's steam made it so as if she was almost floating over him. Dominic kissed first and their tongues began tangling, parrying and thrusting.

Dominic's lips then trailed down a hot path to Bernadette's breast. Taking in the nipple, Big Daddy suckled greedily. Bernadette titled her head back and moaned. After a long sequence, Bernadette dropped her head forward, resting it against his as her hands slid from his backside to the front and down to his cock.

Dominic sang out with a low moan as her hand jerked him, bringing him close to the edge of an orgasm.

Pulling his lips off her breast he moaned, "Bernadette, fuck—" He squirmed as he was about to cum. "Stop—"

Right before he did, Bernadette released it and then braced her hands on his shoulders arching herself up. Dominic's held her as she lowered herself onto his cock until it was sheathed deep inside.

"Wow, Big Daddy—" she purred and began moving slowly, setting the pace. Dominic mimicked, and their bodies were in sync, as their arousal built.

"I love you," she said panting.

"I love you more," he said, kissing her. "You are my life. Fuck—" he couldn't finish saying his words feeling the perfect bending of Bernadette's back and the tensing of her vagina indicating she was close to coming.

"Oh God! Oh God! Fuck me, Dominic. Fuck me. I'm —" Bernadette screamed moving frantically as she strove for her climax.

Dominic thought that if he died right then and there, he would be a very happy man. There was no sight to him of more pleasure than that of his wife coming while being in his arms. She yelled his name as her climax hit, her body bucking and shuddering and that was enough to make him come almost at the same time.

They held each other for several minutes before Bernadette broke the silence between them.

"I could stay here like this forever but I suppose we'd best get out before Anthony and the others rush in here believing we've been attacked."

"No," he joked. "They'll just think we've finally died from all the sex we've been having on this trip."

"Dominic, you're so bad. What would I do without you?" Bernadette said hitting his shoulder. "You're so naughty."

"I am? "He said. "But that's why you love me isn't it?"

"Love you? Where did you get that from?" Bernadette said leaning back. "What makes you think I love you?" She giggled catching the playful look in Dominic's eyes just before he lifted her off him.

"Dominic, what are you doing?"

"This." He carried her and then tossed her into the water.

"Oh, you are a dead man, Dominic Collins," she said, wagging her finger.

"I'm so scared," Dominic said winking. When he lunged forward, Bernadette swam away. Big Daddy began the chase once again.

* * *

Gerard, Amy's husband looked at his watch again, sighing then turned to Amy. "Maybe you should go and get the two lovebirds."

"Me? Why me?"

"Because Dominic won't kill you for interrupting," he said.

"No way—I'm not going?" Amy said.

"Come on, baby—please honey sugar pie? Besides Dominic will have my head if I saw him and Bernadette fucking. I have business dealings with him, you know."

"And what about me? I'm his wife's bestie." Gerard stares at his wife. "No...no... no way...I'm not going. There's no way in hell and back that you can make me."

Gerald stared again resembling a cute puppy.

"Oh, all right. Stop looking at me like that. You owe me, Mr. G. Big time. I want you to—"

"Ok—I'll give you the G treatment tonight. Just go. I'll meet you in the lobby."

Amy put on her coat and headed to the Springs.

* * *

Just as Amy arrived, the doors to the change rooms opened and the couple stepped out.

"Um—Hi," Amy smiled. "Gerard was beginning to worry."

"Really?" Bernadette smiled. "We weren't in there that long, were we?"

"Nearly two hours," Amy said.

"Wow, it really didn't seem that long," Dominic said as they walked back towards the main entrance meeting Gerard. "I hear you were worried about us, bud." Dominic chuckled.

"Huh, me?"

"You didn't send Amy to go in there after us, did you?" Bernadette said nearly laughing at the reaction Amy gave Gerard.

"Let's head back to the hotel," Dominic said as he held out his arm to Bernadette.

"Yes, my love," she said taking his arm. As they went towards the exit, Bernadette turned around seeing Amy and Anthony still standing. "Are you two coming or not?"

Amy looked at Gerard and saw in his eyes what exactly what he was going to say.

"Don't you even!"

"Who me?"

Amy said something under her breath and the couple followed along.

"I can't believe we are almost at the end of our vacation already," Bernadette said as she finished getting ready for the New Year's Eve Ball.

"I know right," Dominic said going into the bedroom to get his shoes.

Meanwhile, Bernadette was looking in the mirror. She usually had a stylist do her hair but she'd given the girls time off for the holidays.

She finished putting on her makeup and then opened her jewelry box taking out the necklace Dominic had bought her for Christmas. After putting it on, she put the box back into the hotel room's safe.

The doorbell rang.

"That's Amy and Gerald," Dominic said as he came up beside her, resting his hands on her. "Are you ready?"

"As I'll ever be," Bernadette turned around kissing him. Taking her hand, Dominic led her to the front door.

* * *

The couples stopped outside the ballroom while Mark ordered his security team to enter first and position themselves. Gerard and Amy preceded them, the two bodyguards on watch, Bill and Carlos, and then followed by Dominic and Bernadette.

"Where's Anthony, Amy?" Bernadette said.

"You know he's upstairs playing online with his friends."

"Oh, okay."

Just as they stepped through the doorway into the ballroom the announcer said, "We'd like to welcome our special guests, Bernadette Collins of Bene and husband Dominic."

The couple stood for a moment in the doorway, accepting the applause that followed the announcement, and then they went into the ballroom.

Bernadette had accepted a flute of champagne when she heard her name being called. Bill and Carlos stepped up to flank her, but when she saw who was running through the crowd, she smiled and motioned them back.

"Bernadette, Bernadette," Kathryn said running forward.

"Well—hello, Kathryn." Bernadette said as she knelt to face the little girl, playing with her curls.

"Excuse me for a moment, my love... I see another young lady who has caught my eye," Dominic said. Bernadette frowned but then smiled when she saw him stop in front of Kathryn and bow.

"May I have the pleasure of this dance, Miss Kathryn," Dominic said. Kathryn giggled and looked back at her mother. Vanessa nodded and smiled with Dominic as he took her daughter's hand and led her out onto the dance floor.

As Dominic began dancing with Kathryn, Vanessa went over to where Bernadette and Amy were.

Bernadette grinned when she saw Kathryn looking up at Dominic.

"Looks like my hubby has stolen another girl's heart," Amy said.

"My husband has that effect on women," Bernadette said watching the two.

"He's so good with her," Vanessa said.

"Yes, he would have made a wonderful father," Bernadette said.

"And he is a fabulous dancer," Vanessa said seeming not to have heard Bernadette's comment.

"You have no idea," Amy said. "I walked in on the two of them one day dancing... Ooh boy!"

"Really?" Vanessa said.

"Yeah," Amy said. "Just wait until they get into it. They're just warming up."

After a few minutes, Kathryn ran back to her mother. "Mommy, Mommy—Mr. Dominic danced with me."

"I saw that sweetie," Vanessa said as she picked her daughter up and hugged her. Looking over her daughter's head, Vanessa said, "Thank you." Dominic gave her a thumbs-up. "How about we go and get something to eat?" Vanessa said to her daughter. "Ok, Mommy."

"Please excuse us."

Once Vanessa and Kathryn had left, Bernadette said to

Dominic, "I see you've stolen another young lady's heart. I knew you were trouble when I first met you."

Dominic laughed, wrapping around Bernadette's waist. "There's only one girl's heart that matters."

"Oh you are such a sweet talker, mister," she said.

"Does this mean I'll get lucky tonight?" he said, his breath tickling Bernadette's ear.

"Oh, it's a pretty safe bet you will, Big Daddy." Bernadette purred looking at him before turning her head.

Bernadette turned back to Amy who was beside her and began sipping from her wine glass. Looking back over her shoulder she spotted Mark standing with Bill against the wall. Turning back to Dominic, she leaned in and whispered something. Dominic leaned in glancing at Amy and then over his shoulder at Mark. He then said, "I'll take care of it."

"Good, my boy."

Dominic squeezed Bernadette's hand and stepped back, going over to stand on the other side of Mark.

He leaned in close and said, "So, are you just going to stand here all night looking at that woman or are you going to ask her to dance?"

"Dominic... I'm working, remember," Mark said.

"Yes, you are and work didn't stop me from dancing for the first time with Bernadette at the company's Christmas party when I was still an employee of Bene."

"And the difference was that you were dancing with the woman you had known for a decade. I wouldn't be."

"Mark—buddy," Dominic said facing him. "It's okay if you want to dance. We have enough detail tonight – go on. It's New Year's Eve and it's okay to have a little fun."

"I—I don't know."

"Mark, I guarantee nothing will happen – relax, buddy. Bill and the others are on guard. Go on—"

Mark appeared to be ready to protest but then said. "Thanks, boss."

"Anytime."

Mark went over to the attractive brunette while Bill leaned over and said, "Geez, I thought he'd never find the nerve to ask that woman to dance."

"Me, either." Dominic chuckled then went back to Bernadette.

"Dance with me, my lady?" he said in her ear.

"Always," she smiled, holding out her hand out.

Chapter Four

As the music played, Dominic pulled Bernadette in closer and she snuggled. She closed her eyes, letting her other senses take over as Dominic led her through the steps. The pressure of his hand on her back felt good. His warmth sept through her body and chased along with her, making her insides tingle. She breathed in his scent of musk and spicy aftershave leaving her giddy.

"Hmm, Mr. Big Daddy's glad to see me. I feel," Bernadette said in his ear.

"You already know," Dominic said moving his lips up to her ear. "I want to fuck my beautiful wife."

"Mmm, what a coincidence because I want to fuck you too, husband," Bernadette said blowing hot air in his ear.

"What do you say we ditch this party and go fuck somewhere?"

"Mmm, that's the best thing you've said all day."

"You're going to have to walk in front of me though."

"And why's that?" Bernadette said giggling, knowing exactly what he meant.

"Hmm, because—" Dominic said. "This hard-on will get us in trouble. Do you want that?"

"Hmm, maybe I do." Bernadette's eyes dropped for a moment. When she lifted them, she was amazed licking her lips. "Oh, you're mine, buddy."

"If we don't go now while this room is full of people... I'm going to have to fuck you right here," he said.

"Oh my, you are a brave man," Bernadette said moving away from the heat. Dominic followed behind her and she faked a smile moving through the crowd.

One of the personal detail, Bill followed them closely to where Gerard and Amy were dancing.

"Having fun you two?" Bernadette said smiling.

"Of course."

"Good. Hubby and I are going to call it a night."

"It's almost midnight...you'll miss the countdown," Amy said. "And the fireworks."

"That's okay, dear. We'll watch them from the balcony." Bernadette said, "Stay and enjoy the party."

When Bernadette and Dominic walked off, Gerard said, "Those two lovebirds can't stop fucking."

Bernadette chuckled. "I wish you did it to me at least half the time, they do."

* * *

After saying their goodnights, the couple headed up to the room. At the door, Bernadette turned back to Bill. "Why don't you head back down to the party and find yourself a nice young lady to dance with."

"I'll try, ma'am." Bill smiled. "If you insist, but I don't think I'd have much luck."

"Oh, and why is that?" Bernadette said, raising her eyebrows, knowing there are women dying to be with anyone who works for her.

"Well, the girl I want is already taken," he said winking and going back down the hall.

"Good night, Bill. Happy New Year."

"Happy New Year, ma'am."

Bernadette closes the door.

"Oh, that Bill is going to give you a run for your money, my love," Bernadette said as she turned back to Dominic.

"Am I in danger of losing my spot in your infatuations, my love?" Dominic said as he took off his jacket.

"Never! You'll always be my number one no matter who sweet-talks me." Bernadette kissed Dominic as she breezed past him.

Just as Bernadette stepped into the parlor, they heard the fireworks from the lawn of the hotel. Bernadette stepped out onto the balcony, shivering, as the starburst of colors peppered the night.

Dominic put his jacket over her shoulders and held her waist pulling her back.

They watched the fireworks until the last one. "Happy New Year, honey."

"Happy New Year, my darling," Bernadette said. Dominic bent over to kiss her.

"Shall we take this inside?"

"Yes, Big Daddy."

* * *

Bernadette slowly awoke, and even without looking at the clock she knew it was still early. Dominic's arms were around her waist and he pulls her back against him.

"Again?" she said as she felt the heat of his cock pressing against her butt.

"Again and again, and again until morning and we're both too tired to move," Dominic said with his hand sliding sensuously up along her thigh.

"Mmm, but it's already morning," Bernadette said as she rolled over, turning until she was facing him. She put her leg over his, hooking her foot behind his butt to pull him closer. "You're a mess," she said after she kissed him.

"Only when it comes to you," Dominic said before running his fingers through her hair and kissing back. Their tongues began a sensual dance, twining together, lunging and retreating.

Dominic caressed each curve and hollow of Bernadette's body and began going lower.

Bernadette moaned when Dominic's finger went inside her. She was wet moaning deeper as his finger slid in and out then moving back up to her clit. Dominic kept stroking, slow and steady.

Bernadette leaned back allowing her hips to move in sync with his thrusting. She then joined Dominic, closing tightly around his hand with hers, as she began rubbing her clit. She moved in slow circles gradually picking up speed while Dominic kept fingering. "Big Daddy—"

Dominic felt Bernadette was about to come. He got on top of her and began stabbing. Bernadette gasped as he slid in and she wrapped her legs around him, locking her ankles together, and moving with him. "Fuck me—Daddy. Ooo, ooo—Yes, yes. Right there, right there—"

Their mouths fused; tongues tangling hungrily, swallowing moans and gasps of pleasure.

With each thrust, Bernadette was nearing a major climax.

Knowing her body as well as his, Dominic knew that she was almost there. He slipped his finger inside, stabbing her with two swords. "Fuck me, Fuck me. Oh! Oh! Oh!" Bernadette's hips bucked and she cried his name as she came. Dominic almost came before Bernadette; he moaned her name as she did his.

They held each other, sharing slow kisses implying it was time for a quick break.

As their slow caresses and kisses continued, it was inevitable that it was time to fuck again. They made love until they came the first hint of dawn appeared on the horizon.

Chapter Five

"Do we have to leave today?" Bernadette sighed leaning back against Dominic as they lay together, her back to his front.

"Yes, dear," Dominic said. "I'm sorry, my love."

"It's alright," she said, taking his hand from where it was and kissing the back of it. "It had to end sometime. And as hard as it is to leave here, it'll be nice to be back home, in our own bed."

"Yes, ma'am," Dominic said.

They turned on the TV and after a quick embrace. The doorbell rang downstairs shattering the moment.

"Damn...What does anyone want this early?" Bernadette said. "I'll get it," she got from under Dominic's arms.

She opened the door and found Gerard and Amy there.

"Good morning," Gerard said. "Sorry to disturb you so early but may Amy and I speak with you both for a few minutes?"

"Of course, come in. Is there something wrong?" Bernadette stepped aside so they both could enter.

"No, no. Nothing like that."

Bernadette led them into the upper parlor when Dominic appeared at the bottom of the staircase, tying the belt of his robe.

"Darling, Gerard, and Amy have something they want to speak to us about," she said.

"Oh, isn't it a holiday to talk business?" he said.

"Well, Dominic. It's—"

"Let me tell him," Gerard began nervously while looking at Amy.

"Dominic, Madam Bernadette.... Anthony and I, well —we got engaged last night..." she said, holding out her left hand to show her diamond ring. "We'd like your blessing."

"Ooh," Bernadette said. "Congratulations, of course, you have it," she said as she embraced Amy. Dominic was grinning as he stepped forward to slap Anthony on the back.

"I told you to do this years ago. Didn't I?"

"Yes, you did." Gerard agreed.

"There's no champagne leftover but we have some brandy," Dominic said going over to the bar. He took the bottle and took out four glasses. Once they each had a glass, Dominic lifted his high to toast.

"To Gerard and Amy, may your lives together be filled with more loving than fighting, more laughter than tears and may you enjoy a long and happy life together."

"Cheers, cheers."

"Thank you," Amy said.

* * *

"Well, we don't want to keep you any longer... I know we all have a lot to do before the cars are ready to leave. We just wanted to share our great news."

"Did you tell Anthony yet?" Bernadette said.

"Yeah, while I was telling him, he was playing his video games."

"That boy—"

"Well, I'm glad you did this. It's been a long time," Bernadette said embracing Amy again. "Congratulations, I'm so happy for you."

"Thank you," Amy said. "It means so much to me to have your blessing."

"Oh, you are very welcome, my dear," Bernadette said. "I hope you know that I look upon you as more than just my partner. You're family."

"Thank you," she said again, moving back to Gerard.

Once Anthony and Amy left, Bernadette turned to her

husband. "As much as I would love to climb back into bed with you, we should probably get ready, the cars will be here before we know it."

"Okay dear," Dominic said as he leaned in to kiss her forehead. "I'll put in a rain check?"

"Oh, absolutely," Bernadette said as she quickly kissed him then headed upstairs to shower and start packing.

* * *

The SUV stopped on the tarmac in front of their private jet.

"Thank you, Walter," Dominic said quietly so as not to wake Bernadette who was sleeping.

"You're welcome, sir, it's been a pleasure. Is there anything else, sir before I get the door for you?"

"No, we're okay. Thanks," Dominic said waiting for Walter to get out. Walter opened the door and before climbing out; Dominic shifted Bernadette so that she was lying on the seat. He got out and then reached in to pull her up and into his arms. She mumbled and as he pulled her close, Dominic kissed her on the forehead.

"Anything else I can do to help?" Walter said as he closed the car door.

"Please see to the bags, Walter, thank you," Dominic said quietly as he carried Bernadette to the plane. He quickly went up the stairs, responding quietly to the pilot's greeting as he reached the top. Dominic carried Bernadette past the main seating area to a large room at the back of the plane. Pushing the door open with his shoulder, he stepped inside the room and went to the bed. Using his free arm, Dominic tugged back the covers and then laid Bernadette down, smiling when she rolled onto her side.

Dominic slipped off her boots then he removed her coat, skirt, and blouse then leaving her in only her slip. Then, he pulled the covers up over her, tucking them in around her.

"Sweet dreams, my love," he said before slipping out of the room and closing the door behind.

He headed back to the main seating area and found the pilot ready. Amy, Gerard, and Anthony were already buckled in. Dominic buckled himself in, giving a nod to his bodyguard Pierre when he was ready.

"Ladies and Gentlemen, thanks for boarding. The weather is clear across the Atlantic. We don't anticipate any problems so our flight time home should be around ten hours." The pilot came out to make a last check before heading to the cockpit.

Once the plane was airborne, Amy and Gerard saw Dominic get up to return to his cabin.

"Stay here with us, buddy. She'll be fine," Gerard said.

"I know but I'm feeling a bit tired as well. See you in a bit"

"Ok. Hey, Gerard, let's head to our quarters. You owe me something, don't you?" Amy said.

Anthony put his hand over his mouth.

"Hey, you stay here and play your little video games, young man. Daddy and Mommy have something to talk about," Amy said.

"Yes, mom."

"Hey, before I go. There's a bottle of old champagne in the galley. It's yours. Go have some. You deserve it," Dominic said smiling.

"Thanks, Bud."

The shades were drawn and Dominic stripped down to his boxers, leaving his clothes draped over an armchair in the corner. He climbed into bed with Bernadette and curled onto her backside. He then pushed back her hair to lean in and say, "I love you" before closing his eyes and joining her dreams.

Alex & Rob

Prologue

Leading up to the New Year's Eve Party

Two weeks ago, Brooke had gone onto Alex's laptop while he was at work to beta read his latest fiction novel.

She clicked on the folder marked *unedited* as she did when Alex would lend her the computer to review his works. This time, she went further and opened another folder inside of *Unedited* marked *For No One's Eyes.*

Brooke was intrigued at the folder's name. The list of titles inside looked okay; some were historical, shifter, fantasy, and contemporary romances. One caught her eye, titled *Santa's Little Helpers.* She began reading and enjoyed Alex's prose; he liked starting things off with a bang but a few pages in, Brooke was caught off guard; the story unfolded into an erotic Christmas fairy tale. The story revolved around a man who had no idea he was half-man, half-elf. As the story unfolded, the female elves were having orgies with the half-elf at Santa's Workshop while he was out delivering presents. Brooke found herself becoming aroused as she read page after page.

She had been so wrapped up in the story she had missed the knock at the door. Her sister-in-law, Jenna showed up for their planned lunch date a few minutes early. Jenna opened the door to a shocking surprise; Brooke was on the couch, Alex's laptop was next to her as she stared at the screen. Brooke's sweatpants were down and she was rubbing her clit. There were also wet spots underneath her.

"Jenna, what are you doing here? My God!"

"Nothing, I'm—" Brooke said hurriedly while pulling up her sweatpants.

* * *

Brooke was embarrassed, explaining what had caused her to play with herself. Jenna wanted to read the story and before long she too was doing the same.

"Please don't tell anyone about this," Brooke said.

"Our secret," Jenna pinky-fingered Brooke. "Email me this story. It sounds so hot."

Brooke emailed the elf story to Jenna and then they went out for lunch.

* * *

As soon as Brooke got home, she started searching on Alex's computer for more stories and began emailing them to Jenna over the next few days. Brooke and Jenna giggled about how hot they were but Brooke started feeling bad about going into Alex's computer to dig them up.

"He's got to be selling them, Brooke. I swear..." Jenna said when she called Brooke to talk about the latest story.

"I know but Alex's so private about everything. I feel so bad..."

"Well, they're hot. Keep them coming. I'll talk to you later, bye." Jenna hung up.

Where the hell is he uploading these naughty stories?

Brooke went through Alex's browser history but it was set to *delete all history* whenever he logged out. After some time, Brooke found an icon in his bookmark toolbar marked *uploads*.

When Brooke clicked the link, an Erotica website came up. The website was free and had a list of categories ranging from couples, to swingers to incest, to paranormal.

Brooke typed in Alex's name to see if he had uploaded under his real name. *Nothing came up*. Then, she looked at the titles of the five stories in Alex's *For No One's Eyes folder*. She chose one and typed the title into the website's search bar. *What the fuck! It's a twenty-book series.*

She texted the website address to Jenna.

"Oh my God!" Jenna replied. "More smut..."

"I'm going to get Alex real good," Brooke replied.

"No, let's have fun with this. Don't say anything."

"You're such a freak. Alex's just got in. Bye," Brooke said hanging up.

Brooke and Jenna had been texting each other the night before the New Year's Eve party about Alex's latest story involving a holiday party and twin sisters who swapped their husbands without their husbands knowing. By the time their party had begun, Jenna already had a good buzz going and Brooke had one, too.

Alex had gotten home late from work to find Brooke dressed, a glass of wine in hand and reading on his laptop. Little did he know Jenna was messaging Brooke about his holiday erotica story.

"I see you're ready to have some fun," Alex said when he put his keys down on the table.

"Yeah, baby I've been waiting for you for hours."

"I'm sorry sweetheart, traffic was bad on the way home.

What are you reading over?" Alex said walking closer to Brooke.

"Ah—nothing just some news about one of the local breweries closing down because of the pandemic. That's all."

Alex embraced Brooke and within an hour, they made it to the party.

Chapter One

The New Year's Eve party at Brooke's sister-in law, Jenna's place had not started yet as Alex and Brooke Jennings knocked on the door. The invitation read it would start at six but as usual they were late, ninety minutes to be exact. Most who were already there were Brooke's older family relatives and a few neighbors.

"How is it that a party starts at six and it takes more than an hour or two to get to it?" Alex asked no one in particular as Brooke's younger sister-in-law, Jenna answered the door.

"People have lives, Alex. Not everyone can be on time all the time. Besides, there are plenty of us already here," Jenna said, smiling at her sister's husband. She gave Brooke a hug first then Alex.

Alex took note of Jenna's firm breasts as she hugged

him, pressing hard against him. She had already had a few drinks before they arrived. "I missed you guys," she said embracing Alex longer than usual.

Alex couldn't keep from thinking how good Jenna's boobs felt. He wiped his forehead and cleared his throat. "We miss you, too, Jenna!"

Brooke smiled as she watched Jenna finally stopped hugging Alex. She was sure Jenna did this on purpose. Jenna winked at Brooke, telling the couple to come inside.

* * *

Jenna's husband Rob was stocking the bar while talking with a neighbor. Alex took a seat at the dining room table as Brooke helped Jenna put out food and soft drinks. Once Alex asked if he could help, they both laughed and told him to just stay seated.

As more people arrived, Alex found himself chatting with a few male members of the family until Brooke walked into the dining room grinning.

"Honey, why don't you tell them about the latest story you published?" Brooke said.

Alex described his story and how it was published. He showed them the Kindle version and one of the women began to read the first paragraph out loud. Jenna's name was mentioned but the story wasn't erotic. Yet, everyone wanted to know more.

"Why don't you tell them about your other story?" Brooke said, grinning again. Alex suddenly knew she had read his erotica stories. "You know, the one about Santa and his elves?"

"What about Santa's Elves?" The others said wanting to know.

"Alex wrote an erotica story about Santa and his little helpers. Right, Alex?" Brooke said as Alex's face reddened.

Brooke walked into the kitchen and chuckled.

"He's beet red. My God! He's going to kill you," Jenna whispered to Brooke. "Hey Alex, let's hear the story," Jenna yelled from the kitchen.

"I—I don't know what you're talking about..."

"Wow, it must be something because you're as red as Mars, Alex," Aunt Margaret laughed, "Tell us, Brooke, what's it about?"

"Oh, Santa's Elves having orgies while Santa's out delivering gifts," Brooke said.

* * *

The more Brooke talked, the redder Alex's face had gotten. Everyone was laughing as he remained speechless. Jenna walked inside the living room and stood behind Alex. Everyone at the table was giving Alex ideas for his story; *what should happen next or how it would come about.*

"Santa walked in and caught them having sex on his spare sled on the night of Christmas Eve. My God!" Aunt Magaret yelled. "Keep going, Brooke. We have to hear more."

Everyone laughed.

Jenna laughed leaning forward, placing her wondrous tits on Alex's shoulder. The firmness and weight sent shock waves through Alex's body as everyone kept laughing.

"Sounds like you might have a bestseller..." Becky laughed.

"I just might," Alex said.

Meanwhile, Jenna's breasts were still pressed on Alex's right shoulder. Alex reached down and back with his hand to grab the back of Jenna's left calf and instead, he touched the V between her legs.

Alex froze as everyone continued to talk not seeing what just happened. Jenna giggled knowing what Alex had done. She squeezed her legs together trapping his arm. Then, she slid down an inch allowing more of her breasts to press into Alex's shoulder while his elbow pressed harder into her crotch. Jenna angulated up and down a few times in a way no one noticed but Alex.

* * *

As the hilarious conversation was ending, Jenna got up off of Alex's shoulder and let go of his arm. She walked away as the women at the table continued gossiping about the book, making more plots up as they went along. Alex watched Jenna walked away and his wife Brooke smiled noticing his reaction from the kitchen.

Chapter Two

The night went on and after the meal and a few drinks, people began to leave. Aunt Margaret and others asked for a copy of the story on their way out.

"I'll send it to you," Brooke told them as the women laughed exiting the front door.

Alex got up from the table as Brooke left to head towards the kitchen. "Hey, we need to talk."

Brooke followed him into the shed where it was dark and they were alone.

"Why did you tell them about my story?" Alex asked.

"Alex, women have desires too. We like to read erotica more than men do. I bet if you were to write more, people will buy more." Brooke told him.

"That was my secret," Alex said as Brooke kissed him with his back to the door.

“I need to go clean up. I’ll be back,” Brooke said kissing him again.

* * *

Alex felt embarrassed about tonight’s gossip. He leaned against the side of the door in the shed and suddenly felt his butt being palmed. Alex thought it was Brooke. Seconds later, his crotch was next to be palmed.

"Mmm.”

"Brooke, not while people can see,” Alex said as he turned seeing Jenna behind him. "So you like writing about women taking control and swapping husbands, huh?" Jenna said.

"How do you know that?”

“Brooke found your naughty stories and we've been reading them." She chuckled, her lips close to Alex’s ear. Her warm breath blew inside it as she whispered.

Alex’s manhood twitched as Jenna continued holding his crotch. He closed his eyes as her breath against his ear and then his neck soothed him.

Jenna then released Alex’s hard cock and left him in the shed alone. Alex took a deep breath relishing the scent that Jenna had left behind. *Damn, she’s hot!*

* * *

Alex walked back to the kitchen to find Brooke helping to clean up. She had been drinking as much as Jenna had so the clean-up took a little while longer. Alex was told to leave the kitchen. Sitting at the table by himself, Alex was trying to bring his raging hard-on under control. The rest of the guests had left leaving Jenna, Rob, Brooke and Alex in the house. Jenna and Rob's eighteen-year old son, Justin was staying the night with his great-grandmother.

Once the cleaning was done, Brooke was ready to leave. Rob shook Alex's hand as Jenna and Brooke hugged. Jenna turned to give Alex a hug goodbye as Rob went to give Brooke the same. Brooke kissed Rob's lips as she wrapped her arms around his neck. Jenna smiled seeing what Brooke had done. Jenna stepped up to Alex wrapped her arms around his neck and planted her lips on his.

Alex's cock got hard as Jenna's tits were pressed against his chest. Jenna's tongue forced its way down Alex's mouth as she began grinding against him. Her hand dropped to his crotch, palming it and then rubbing it. She moaned low enough that she could not be heard by anyone except Alex. Alex reached down to cup her buttcheeks which made Jenna pant.

* * *

Moments later, Alex noticed Brooke pulling Rob into the living room, still kissing him. He wanted to say something but he could not. Brooke's hand was around his cock. At some point, she had unzipped his pants and pulled it out. Alex lost sight of them as they went further inside.

"Shouldn't we join them, brother," Jenna said, her hand was still grasping his crotch.

"I guess so," Alex moaned.

Jenna led Alex into the living room where Brooke was kneeling in front of Rob on the couch. Rob's pants and boxers were around his ankles and his cock was at the back of Brooke's throat as she sucked him. Brooke was bobbing her head up and down on Rob's cock and I was astonished.

"Brooke, what the fuck?" I shouted.

"Shut up Alex and enjoy! You wanted to be naughty, right?" Brooke gasped between breaths.

"But—"

"Don't say anything..."

Chapter Three

"Look at you, Brooke. You still got skills, don't you?" Jenna said as she pushed Alex on to the couch next to Rob.

Jenna unfastened Alex's pants, pulling them down with his underwear to his ankles. She smiled as Alex's cock almost slapped her in the face. She started jerking it as she looked first at Rob who had his head back enjoying the blowjob Brooke was giving him.

"Enjoying yourself tonight honey. This stays between us," Jenna said to Rob as she started giving Alex a hand job.

"Uh huh," Rob said barely able to speak.

"Good, because I'm going to enjoy my big brother-in-law here," Jenna said as she took Alex's cock into her mouth to the root.

Jenna began sucking and licking the head of Alex's

cock as she looked up at him, smiling. The sparkle in her eyes was driving Alex crazy.

"Like what she's doing to you?" Brooke asked from beside Jenna as she looked at her husband. She continued jerking Rob as she spoke.

Alex couldn't speak as Jenna bit down on the head of his cock. Brooke smiled as she went back to sucking Rob. Alex reached forward to pull on Jenna's top. She raised her arms as he pulled it off. Then, she unfastened her bra allowing her 36 double-D tits to say hello. A moment later Brooke's almost identical-sized tits were saying hello as well.

"I'm cumming." Rob moaned and seconds later Brooke was gulping down spurt after spurt of Rob's orgasm. Cum ran down the side of her mouth as some escaped. Brooke continued licking and sucking Rob's cock as she got every last drop.

"Done already?" Jenna asked as she looked over, taking her mouth off Alex's cock and now using with her hand.

Alex seized that moment to pull away from Jenna. He jumped off the couch, pushing her forward. Jenna had unbuttoned her pants while she sucked his cock and had been fingering herself. Now Alex had her pinned against the couch as he slid her pants down to her knees. He licked the crack of her ass as Jenna continued to suck.

Jenna and Alex's fuck session was making Rob's cock hard again.

Alex then slid his fingers into Jenna's pussy, she was dripping wet as he fingered her while rubbing her clit. He drove his fingers as deep as he could, twisting and screwing away. A moment later, his fingers found her spot and Brooke began to writhe on the couch. He pressed hard against her G-spot and began to flick against it. Loud moans could be heard all through the house.

Alex looked over at Rob who had stripped Brooke and had her sitting on the couch, legs spread. He was licking and eating her pussy as his finger danced on her clit and in her pussy. Brooke left a wet spot on the couch as she squirmed under Rob's assault. She was moaning and groaning as she pushed back against Rob's fingers and face, both in action.

Jenna started moaning as she started to cum. Her pussy squeezed his fingers tight as her legs bound together. She was trying to push Alex's hand away from her pussy, breathing hard as her juices flowed onto the side of the couch.

Alex pulled his fingers out and pushed his leg between hers and edged forward. Brooke slid her legs apart and Alex took that as his invitation; he place the head of his cock against her opening.

Jenna turned her head, about to say something as Alex drove right into her tight young wet pussy. Jenna squealed as Alex hit the root deep inside, making Jenna forget what she was trying to say. Alex started ramming hard and fast and Jenna moaned each time he bottomed out in her. Alex picked up the pace as Jenna began to push back against his cock.

A loud slap landed on Jenna's ass cheek. It was Brooke who had reached over and slapped Jenna's ass. Rob, seeing that his wife was getting fucked badly, stood up and buried his cock in Brooke. Alex was pounding Jenna hard and deep as she moaned and screamed. Brooke began to moan as well as her brother-in-law Rob pounded her pussy as well. Alex was going faster and faster in Jenna and Rob picked up the pace with Brooke, too.

Brooke let out a loud moan and then scream "Oh, Oh, Oh! Fuck, I'm coming..."

* * *

Meanwhile, Jenna's pussy was dripping cream on Alex's cock and balls as he continued pounding her. Moments later, Jenna was squirming again up and down ejaculating more Alex's cream-coated balls. In the back of his mind for years, he had fantasized how Jenna would feel with his cock inside her. Now, it was a reality.

Suddenly, Jenna yelled as her pussy gripped Alex's cock tightly. Alex felt his sensation as his cock began to tingle. He knew it was too late as his cock erupted deep inside Jenna's pussy. She moaned and groaned as his hot cum spurted over and over into her. Alex continued to pound her but at a slower pace. He tried to stay inside Jenna's pussy as long as he could, wanting to cherish it as long as he could.

* * *

Next to him on the couch, Rob moaned as Brooke's legs wrapped around his back, pulling him deeper into her wet pussy. Rob, within seconds of changing positions, emptied his balls inside Brooke. Brooke continued to hold Rob in place as she rubbed her clit. Moments later, she moaned as she came on his cock. Her cum oozed out on Rob's cock as Alex and Jenna watched.

* * *

Jenna brought Alex back to her, easing forward up onto the back of the couch as everyone's cum dripped out onto the couch. Alex sat back, onto the floor, tired. Rob joined him. Brooke turned around to look at them, smiling. Cum stains wetted the couch's cover and Alex and Jenna's was trailing down towards the floor.

"We can't let this delicious cum go to waste," Brooke said as she rose up.

Alex looked at Rob who seemed to think they were

both going to get their cocks sucked again. Instead, Brooke turned towards Jenna. Without saying anything, she buried her face between Jenna's thighs, lapping up Alex's and Jenna's cum as it poured from her pussy. Brooke then slid her finger inside causing Jenna to moan heavily.

Smiling, Rob stood up. He climbed onto the couch where his wife sat, her legs spread wide while Brooke was eating her out. Brooke had her eyes closed as Rob reached over to pull her head towards his cock. She opened her eyes as a moan escaped her lips. Rob pushed his cock into her mouth, stifling her.

Alex enjoyed watching his wife eat Jenna out while sucking his brother-in-law's cock. He got up behind Brooke and buried his into her cum-drenched pussy.

"Oh my..." were Brooke's only words as she tried to catch her breath.

* * *

Jenna was squirming on the couch playing with herself, she she had orgasm after orgasm while Rob was fucking Brooke's face. Alex drove deep into Brooke as Rob moaned ready to come again. Seconds later, he pulled his cock out of his Brooke's mouth and shot his load all over her tits and in her hair. Alex was almost there and Jenna sensed it so she pulled Brooke off him. Brooke fell backward and Alex did as well, onto his back. His cock glistened with both sister-in-laws' cum coating it. Jenna rolled off the couch onto the floor on top of Alex.

"I want you to cum all in my mouth, big brother. Give it all to me," she said as she took his cock into her mouth.

Jenna sucked Alex's cock as Rob and Brooke sat down on the couch, cuddling and kissing. It didn't take Jenna long to make Alex cum. His cock twitched and she pulled it out of her. Then, she pulled Alex over the top of her and aimed his cock straight at her mouth. After that, she started jerking it and licking its head. Finally, it happened. Alex exploded. Jenna held Alex's cock several inches from her mouth, so Brooke and Rob could watch the show.

Several long spurts landed on her tongue and in her mouth. The last few hit Jenna in the face, her chin and then onto her tits. Jenna bent Alex's cock down onto her tits as she rubbed her nipples with the head.

"Well, that was fun." Brooke said which caused all four to burst out in laughter.

"Yes it was." Jenna said. "Care to stay the night?"

"Why not? It's late," Brooke replied.

Chapter Four

Alex was half-wake after an incredible dream. The dream was so real; he dreamt of Brooke and Jenna rimming and sucking him off. A muffled voice caused him to open his eyes. Between his legs, his sister-in-law, Jenna kneeled, his cock in her mouth.

"About time you woke up, I needed this hours ago," she whispered as she started sucking.

Jenna, for a few minutes, sucked Alex and then got up to ride him. She began moaning different words as Brooke began yelling in the other room.

"Fuck me!" Brooke screamed. "Fuck this pussy! Drive that big dick in me, Robbie!"

"Brooke and Rob are having fun it sounds like," Jenna moaned as she rode on Alex's cock. "She called him, Robbie, that's a first."

“Yes, they must be,” Alex said chuckling.

Alex then reached up and grabbed Jenna's tits. kneading them as he squeezed closer to her nipples. He pulled her left tit down to suck on the nipple. “Fuck!” Jenna panted as she doubled her speed riding his cock. “I'm about to cum...” She moaned, seconds later drenching Alex's cock with her juice. Seconds later, Jenna slumped over onto Alex's chest breathing heavy. Alex did not stop, he continued fucking Jenna from the side riding her to another orgasm just two minutes later. The scent of sex was starting to overtake the room.

"Fuck me harder,” Jenna yelled. "Fuck me like this is yours, daddy,” she panted as she tried to catch her breath.

Alex pushed her off of him on to the bed face down. He got on his knees as he pulled Jenna up onto hers and shoved his cock back into her pussy as she tried to raise up.

"Harder!" Jenna screamed as Alex pounded.

Alex spread her ass cheeks and Jenna was squirming under him as he looked down at her hole. The action brought the loudest moans he ever heard. The good morning wood made it awhile before Alex would come.

As he drove in and out, Alex tried putting the tip of his finger into her ass.

"Oh no you don't. That's off limits." Jenna moaned.

Alex continued to fuck her but didn't remove his finger. Jenna hadn't push his hand away either. He drove deeper into Jenna and tried to slip his finger into her ass up again, then paused. Jenna was moaning even more now as his finger touched her hole.

"Didn't I say that's off limits?" Jenna moaned but smiling.

"It feels good, doesn't it?"

"Mmm, no comment," She moaned. "I told you that's off limits."

"Then maybe this is even more off limits." Alex said as he put two fingers on her hole.

"Mmm, still off limits, buddy..." Jenna moaned.

Alex had both fingers right on her hole and it was driving Jenna crazy. His fingers didn't enter inside her but it felt like it to Jenna. Meanwhile, Brooke was moaning as loud as Jenna was in the other room. Jenna's pussy squeezed Alex's cock as if never to let it go.

"Off limits, I said. Why are you not listening," Jenna said as her pussy clenched tighter feeling Alex's fingers poke in and out of her hole but not entering.

"Oh my God! You're going to make me come..." Jenna's asshole tightened around his fingers as she came on his cock. She breathed heavily as she was hit seconds later by another orgasm. "

Alex spit on her ass allowing a pool to form over Jenna's asshole.

"Off-limits, I said," Brooke tried to say again as she rubbed her clit.

Alex then pulled his cock out of her and pushed it into her ass.

"Whoa!" Jenna screamed. "Off fucking limits." She cried.

He shoved his cock harder this time as Jenna's ass opened up and invited his cock all the way in. His balls slapped against her pussy and hand as she fingered her clit.

"Fuck!" Jenna yelled. "Fuck your hard cock!"

Jenna was moaning and screaming; she was an animal in heat, wanting it all.

"Oh, I feel you throbbing!" Jenna said. "Cum in my ass! Fuck! Cum in my ass! Fill it up!"

Alex within seconds of Jenna's pants unloaded and Jenna kept riding back and forth until he slowed down.

* * *

"Wow! What a way to start the New Year!" Jenna laughed.

Alex moved his head closer to her. Jenna then pulled him in for a long wet, french kiss.

"You were good."

"You were, too."

"I'm so beat. Let's go back to bed."

"I'm up. I'll see you in a bit."

"Ok, Alex." Jenna closed her eyes.

Chapter Five

Jenna fell asleep shortly after and Alex pulled the blanket over her as he got up to shower. He heard Brooke and Rob going at it again, Brooke screaming as a loud slap resounded from the bedroom.

"My God! What a day!"Alex said relishing the hot water as it dripped down his body. He stood under the shower for what seemed over an hour. When he stepped out of the bathroom, he heard nothing. He guessed Brooke and Rob had ceased their fucking for now.

Alex put on some clothes and headed downstairs. The master bedroom door was closed as he walked by. He smiled imagining Jenna had joined Brooke and Rob. As he entered the kitchen, he saw Jenna at the stove cooking breakfast.

"You must be hungry," Alex said. "I thought you were asleep."

"Oh, I'm hungry all right. Rob and Brooke are sleeping, I don't want to disturb them," Jenna said as she turned the stove top off.

Leaning over the counter, she pulled the robe up to reveal she was naked. She looked back over her shoulder.

"Well... I had a long taste, I want a quickie before breakfast."

Alex dropped his pants. His cock popped out and he shoved Jenna into the counter. She moaned as the water in the sink was running.

"Fuck me harder," Jenna panted.

Alex started ramming Jenna's pussy until she could hardly breathe. Groans and moans escaped her lips and she was pushing back with every thrust. A minute later, an enormous orgasm rocked Jenna from head to toe. Alex caught Jenna from falling but continued driving into her. A minute later, his cock exploded in her pussy as they both were bent over the counter.

"Wow!" Jenna breathed. "That was even better the second time around. Can we go for another one before my kid comes home?" She chuckled.

"Maybe," Alex said as he straightened up.

"Go shower again handsome while I finish breakfast. I'll be up shortly," Jenna said.

* * *

Alex went back to the guest bathroom to shower again. He heard the master bedroom door open as he climbed into the shower. Brooke then appeared at the bathroom door, smiling.

"Well, does this measure up to any of your stories?" She asked as she moved towards the shower door.

"Surpasses all of them," Alex said as Brooke climbed into the shower. She washed her face before turning to kiss Alex.

"You don't know how long Jenna and I have been planning this," Brooke said. "I found your stories and the ones you posted online. Brooke caught me fingering myself when we were to have lunch. After that, we would read them together throughout the day and night and things took off from there..."

"So that was what you were doing for the past few weeks?"

"Well, yeah. You were busy working and writing your stories and I was busy being a homebody and reading them," Brooke said.

"So..." Alex said kissing Brooke. "Where do we go from here..."

"Let me show you..."

Brooke dropped to her knees and took Alex's cock

into her mouth. She sucked it until he was hard again. She then stood up, turned around and bent over. Alex shoved his cock into his wife's pussy and they made love in the hot steamy shower for almost an hour.

Chapter Six

Nearly, an hour later, Alex and Brooke came downstairs in towels to find Rob sitting at the table naked.

"Where's Jenna?" Brooke asked.

"Taking a shower. It seems that she's been in there all morning."

"So, what's next...we've done everything?" Alex said.

"Ever try DP?" Rob suggested.

"I'm not sure if I'm up for that. You guys have worn me out," Brooke said. "Let's see if Jenna is okay with that—Hey Jen..." Brooke yelled.

Jenna didn't hear her.

"Who said anything about Jenna?" Alex said as he reached for Brooke's hand.

"Oh no you don't, my ass is off limits," Brooke giggled

as she ran into the living room followed by Alex and then Rob.

"Come to daddy, mama..." Alex said.

"No, Alex. You're such freaks, my God! When do you stop?"

* * *

Brooke was on the couch with a pillow over her lap. Alex sat beside her, pulling her on top of him. His cock slid easily into her. Alex then gestured for Rob to come over. Rob started caressing one of Brooke's tits as Alex slid in and out of her. Moments later, Brooke felt Rob's cock sliding in her ass, she let out a moan that rocked the house. "Fucccccckkkk!"

* * *

Alex and Rob had come quickly and Brooke was completely drained. Jenna hadn't come back downstairs, so Rob went up and found her asleep in bed. He curled up with her and soon did the same. Alex and Brooke showered again before going back to the guestroom to take a quick nap.

Chapter Seven

Alex and Brooke were awaken by their nephew's laughs. They quickly got dressed and came out finding Jenna and her son playing a card game at the kitchen table.

"Good morning," Jenna said. "You two slept late after the party." She grinned.

"Unbelievable, what a New Year's Eve it was!" Alex said yawning.

"I bet. You must not have wanted to wake up," Brooke said.

"If I could go back to that little ole dream right now, I would." Alex grinned at Jenna.

"Where's Rob?" Brooke said still feeling a tingling sensation between her legs and ass."

"Still asleep. I hear you three played a game of twister." Jenna said, grinning.

"Yes, we did. I know Rob and I enjoyed it. Did you honey?" Alex asked.

"It's not worth repeating," Brooke said as she couldn't stop smiling.

"I may have to try playing that game one day—maybe next year," Jenna said.

"Oh mom, aren't you too old for Twister? Even my friends and I don't play it anymore. That game is for old people," Justin said.

"Just because you come from a different generation doesn't mean you can't play old games." Jenna told Justin.

"Well, I'm up for Twister anytime you are," Alex told Jenna.

"We'll have to make plans then," Jenna said grinning.

"I guess I'll leave that up to you guys," Brooke said.

"Brooke, can you take over playing my hand, I need to put a load of laundry in?" Jenna said.

"Sure," Brooke said taking Jenna's place at the table after Jenna stood up.

"Mind if Alex helps?" Jenna asked.

"Be my guest," Brooke said.

Alex kissed his wife.

"Do what Jenna tells you," Brooke said.

* * *

Alex followed Brooke into the small laundry room at

the far end of the house. She was wearing a long skirt and blouse. She smiled as she bent over to pick up a pile of clothes from the floor. She put them in the washer before closing the lid and turning on the machine.

"Now," Jenna said as she hoped up on the dryer. "You have some eating to do. So get on with it, mister." Jenna pulled her skirt up to her waist and Alex moved between her legs as his tongue teased her clit. He slipped a finger into her pussy which brought a quick slap to the back of his head.

"No fingers. Only tongue."

Alex licked and nibbled her pussy and clit for a few minutes before Jenna came. She was so hypersensitive that breathing on her clit probably made her cum. She slid off the dryer and kneeled to unzip Alex's pants. She deepthroated him, moaning as loud as the she could.

Jenna stood up, turned to face the dryer just as Justin called for his mom. Alex put his cock back into his pants and zipped up as Jenna fixed herself. She walked past Alex to see what Justin wanted.

"Mom, we have karate today. Are you going to take us or is Dad?" Justin asked. "Aunt Brooke said she had to head out soon."

Alex remembered that Brooke had to meet her mother for lunch.

The fun was now over.

"I'll take you, sweetheart. Your dad had a long night.

Give me a few minutes. You go get your things and meet me down in the car in five," Jenna told her son.

"Ok, mom."

* * *

Brooke and Alex walked into the kitchen as Jenna was getting straightening up.

"Sorry, sis, I have to go meet Mom today," Brooke apologized.

"Don't be sorry. We'll get together again soon," Jenna said.

They kissed goodbye and then Jenna turned to Alex and gave him a long passionate kiss. They walked out of the house together. Jenna got into her car as Alex and Brooke got into theirs. they waved goodbye as they pulled away from the house.

"Well, that was fun," Brooke said.

"Yes, it was. You two sure made my night." Alex said.

"Our night." Brooke corrected. "Don't think it won't happen again. I know you want more."

"Next year, my love," Alex said as they drove home.

Vladimir & Natalia

Chapter One

It's cold in Moscow.

It's 3:15 p.m. in the afternoon and it's chilly. But Natalia can barely keep up with the sweat rolling down her temples and bubbling on her tee. Every time she wipes it up, another bead rolls down the opposite temple, she's chasing sweat and honestly, it's working her up.

Natalia's hot, hungry, thirsty, and just want to jump into her hot tub a few feet away and never come back up. Just let me peel off my clothes, my skin because God, I'm feeling sweaty today.

Where the hell is Vladimir?

Natalia finished rollerblading on the coldest day of the year. Her repair man, Vladimir had pestered her about coming over early, and Natalia realized why. It was Valentine's Day. Vladimir called her saying he was helping out his father at his shop for a few hours and would be by.

* * *

When Vladimir's blades skidded to a stop outside Natalia's back gate, she looked up from reading the latest issue of Art World, grinned and jumped up from her lounge chair to unlock the gate and embrace him.

Young Vladimir was so strong and he knew it. Natalia loved it when he cracked her back whenever she said she had an ache. It hurt but felt so good and she often wanted another before he left to go home.

Natalia grunted into his ear, causing him to laugh. He kissed her on the cheek as he pressed down on her lower back.

"Stop it. You know what that does to me?"

Vladimir did it again and then went lower to her buttocks. His dimpled cheeks reddened and Natalia looked up at him.

"Come inside before we get in trouble. We have work to do," Natalia said.

Vladimir giggled as he came in.

"Just got back from helping Nana. Man, it's freaking cold out," Vladimir said.

"You ain't lying."

Vladimir took out some packets of folded sandpaper from his back pockets.

"How can I help you this afternoon again, Gaspazah?" Vladimir said chuckling and remembering the first time he met Natalia when he was hired to do some work at her house. Every time Natalia brought it up, he'd tell her, "Just wait," "Everything will be fine." That phrase kept Natalia up at night.

Occasionally, Vladimir teased her by saying, "If I sand it down for you, you're going to drool over me while I do all the work. It won't help my concentration, Natalia."

"Well, that's why I brought you in?" Natalia replied.

"For my looks or craft?"

"Both."

Natalia closed the gate and Vladimir walked inside to get them some Coronas before he started working. This time he remembered to bring the limes, as she always fussed about drinking it straight.

Chapter Two

Natalia's sweating and bent over the picnic table, her biceps are killing her, and she's rubbing sandpaper back and forth on a part that just won't smoothen. Vladimir said, "Keep working on it," as he'd left the backyard, barely sweating. But he'd smelled like a brute and Natalia was glad he had left her alone for a bit. She didn't know how much more she could take of his body odor sabotaging her.

"No more limes," Vladimir said coming back with a smirk, Natalia saw the bowl he was holding behind his back.

"You little shit," She crossed her arms, and Vladimir giggled. He put the bowl on the table and set the bottles down, loosened his grip before plucking one from the bunch and pulling out a switchblade.

Vladimir knew how to cut them just right. His bartending days during his Starving Artist Period had served him well, and he knew how to angle the tip of the lime and wedge it in, pushing it in with just enough force that it doesn't bunch up at the opening and go nowhere. He warned Natalia endlessly about the bad burns from the sun if she doesn't wash her hands when the lime squirts up on her, but she's never seen him wash his own.

The lime popped into the bottle with a fizzle. Natalia watched the juice mingling with the beer and it looked wavy, delicious. Vladimir stuck his fingers in his mouth and sucked the juice off looking at Natalia's face.

"Thanks," she said.

Natalia waited for him to load a lime into his bottle. She watched him repeat the whole process, his fingers lingered in his mouth a little bit longer and Natalia watched until they clinked bottles.

Vladimir's arms were crossed watching Natalia chug it down, she didn't care she'll probably be drunk in minutes because it was cold. She needed something to heat her up.

"If you don't slow down, you're going to throw up," Vladimir said when Natalia kept drinking. She wanted to say something about the vein that was popping in Vladimir's neck while he was working. It's still there, resting wrapped around a tendon. He does it when he's excited Natalie noticed.

Natalia popped another bottle off her lips when she put down her bottle with a third of the beer remaining. Vladimir whistled and shook his head.

"You're looking really sweaty in the cold," he said.

"Well, you forgot that our ancestors were tucked away in the mountains high up. We didn't have this climate change bullshit the Americans keep talking about," Natalia said swirling her beer around and watching the lime bob up and down.

Vladimir chuckled and smacked her hard on the right flank before he put his drink down on the seat of the table. He picked the sandpaper back up. The jolt of electricity that struck through Natalia's core when his big, calloused hand touched her jean shorts was galvanizing.

"You want this finished by before six, right? I've got a Valentine's date! And I need to shower," Vladimir said like he was the one in control, not looking up at Natalia.

But he's only in control on the outside. Natalia had Vladimir in check since the first time he started working at her home. Natalia was divorced with no children and the house she received in alimony was always in need of repairs.

Vladimir tried to fuck Natalia the first time he worked at her home, but she rejected his advance. Soon, it became a game between them, how much Vladimir could get away with, teasing Natalia, before she would either give in a little or yell at him to fuck off and slam the door in his face.

She'd say, "This is the last job I'll ever give you."

He'd reply, "At your service, anytime" and walk off. His peals of laughter haunted her those nights when she laid in bed. Natalia got herself off saying his name until she fell asleep.

Chapter Three

Natalia never gave in. It was the unspoken rule; take it to the edge, get incredibly close, and then Natalia would yell and Vladimir would laugh. Sometime's they'd share a joint and go get food after he finished his job.

But today Natalia wants to give in, right now as Vladimir's bent over the table, working at the spot she couldn't get earlier, smoothing it over with fast, hard flicks of his wrist. The sounds went going directly to Natalia's pussy. She felt it tingling, wet over his grunts and the sweat dripping off his nose. The wood's dust rising aroused her like sprinkles on a cake.

Vladimir's shoulders were pulling at the tight fabric of his tank top and Natalia's tongue was probing the opening of her beer bottle absentmindedly. Her stomach was filled with Corona, she can't drink anymore, but she wanted to.

But she wanted something in her mouth or she would do something crazy. She felt it, between her legs, swelling up with anticipation. Natalia was tired of playing with herself to the thought of her repairman.

Her late husband never fully satisfied her, and she knew why. He was older and acted like he was the boss of everything. With Vladimir, she knew she had full control. He was twenty years younger, innocent and no one would suspect her fulfilling her lust with him. The only thing she needed to do was tame and groom him. He was a work-in-progress.

Meanwhile, Vladimir was sweating bullets over her picnic table while sanding it down, doing all the work as Natalia watched. She wanted to prostrate herself in front of him, swipe the beer off the table and slam her hands on the smooth wood. She wanted to stick her ass out and look up at him with bedroom eyes, tell him to take her now. She wanted Vladimir to stand behind her and unzip his dingy jeans, his skin rough from the sandpaper, shove his fingers inside of her and then follow it up with his cock. Natalia's seen how big it is from his jean's imprint and doesn't think she can take it but she wants to try anyway. She wanted Vladimir to pump into her hard and fast, making her regret drinking her beer so fast and chastising her for it, calling her a bad woman and smacking her ass again. He then would tell her she did this to herself, she had to take it now.

Vladimir looked up at Natalia with his mouth gaped

open a little, and for a split second, she thought it's because he's reading her mind.

"What are you doing over there? Didn't I tell you I'll be doing all the work?" He licked the sweat on his upper lip and Natalia gripped her beer tighter with her bony fingers. "You're watching me like I said."

"That's not fair! I helped!" Natalia said knowing how loud her voice is that she's a little buzzed.

Vladimir laughed. "You helped with a quarter of it, yeah. You did the finer grit because it doesn't require as much strength, but I swear, it took you so long I could have sanded circles around you."

"Well, why do you think I hired you?"

Vladimir laughed loudly. Natalia saw his Adam's Apple bobbing in his throat and want to bite it and suck on it.

"So you could check me out," He said smirking, then returning to his work. "If you're just going to stand there, can you at least hand me my beer?"

It's not even three feet from him and Natalia gritted her teeth.

* * *

Vladimir was sanding hard, pressing down roughly with the meaty part of his palm, rubbing in the sandpaper and twisting a little at it, working at it so much Natalia knew it's because he's thinking of other things just like she is.

Natalia picked up his Corona, seeing he only took three fucking sips. The lime was just sitting there, wasted.

She walked over to him and held the beer over his shoulders and turned it upside down.

The beer pours over him fast before the lime stops up the neck a little, and then it started trickling, glutting out of the bottle. Vladimir hasn't even motioned besides the cessation of his hand on the table.

He didn't turn around and Natalia's blood started boiling. She hoped he's angry with her, wanting to rile him up like he does to her. She knew it's part of the game but she's in her mid-forties now in her peak, and in prime shape to fuck. She exercises every day and is sexually competent. All she imagined was slamming Vladimir down on the grass and riding him until he cried like a stupid college kid. She wanted to wring his neck and make him see stars when he cums.

Vladimir stood up slowly and Natalia followed him with the beer pouring. He turned around seeing it was spilling down his chest. Natalia looked at his pecs through his tank top, his nipples hardening at the cool liquid.

She held it there, against his chest, the rim of the bottle on his birthmark, and he held her gaze, serious, sharp and heavy until the bottle emptied.

"What the fuck was that for?

Natalia smirked.

"We're going to need to take showers, anyway, right, Mister Bossman?"

Vladimir stepped forward and closed the space between them. Natalia was so swollen between her legs that the denim was making her ache.

"What'd you call me?" He said, snatching the bottle from her and throwing it in the grass, where it thumped and rolled away. His eyes didn't leave hers, and she leveled with him, inches shorter and much lighter but what she lacked in height and weight she made up for in attitude.

"What, Mister Bossman?" She jerked her eyebrows up, tilting her head back.

"You're really asking for it."

Natalia shrugged.

She's never shrugged. This is the moment where she slapped his meaty bicep telling him to go away or she's calling the police. But this time she shrugged and watched Vladimir's expressions change from challenged to surprised to aroused.

"Say it again," he said. The sweat was beaded where he shaved his mustache his morning, the hair was prickling back up leaving a dark cast on his skin. Natalia wanted to feel it on her tongue, between her legs.

"Say what?"

"*It.*"

Natalia licked her lips and Vladimir's eyes zoomed in

on her mouth before coming back up to her eyes.

"Vladimir," She whispered, and his eyes bugged a little at his name. "I want you to fuck me, right here, on this stupid fucking table, and make me come, as many times as the years I've been on Earth." She knew she just set the tone for the roughest fucking she'll ever receive.

"Well, if that's what the princess wants," He said in a low tone. "I guess Mister Bossman has to give the lady what she wants."

* * *

Before Natalia knew what was going to happen, Vladimir's grabbed her by the waist and flipped their positions, spun her around, and she's facing the picnic table, catching herself on it with her hands so she doesn't fall.

He dead-legged her in the backs of both knees, pushing them with his own knee to make her kneel on the seat of the table, and his rough hands ran up and down her back, catching on her shirt and pushing and pulling at it.

Natalia's skin was clutched in his hands. Then, Vladimir brought them down the small swell of her ass, cupped it and squeezed hard, pinching her through her jeans. Natalia didn't know how he did it but she didn't care, it's making her whine and he's groaning.

Vladimir's fingers slipped down past her cheeks and between her thighs and they both gasped. She felt a jolt again, it's a dull throb this time as he rubbed his fingers against the denim and pressed in a little.

"Fuck, you're wet, aren't you," he said. Natalia loved how ragged his young voice was, feeling how hard he is against her cheek as he grinds on her slowly. Natalia rotated her hips up and back and stuck her ass out to meet his thrusts.

Natalia knelt on the table with her ass up in the air, her head slowly fell to rest on her forearms, having her ass and her pussy played with relentlessly. Vladimir's there in his work boots and dirty jeans, his shaved head glistened in the wintery sunlight from his sweat, touching her all over.

Vladimir took the hand that wasn't between her legs up to her spine and gripped the hair at the base of her neck, tugging on her shoulder-length curls just enough to make her moan. He then yanked her head back a little. She's staring up at the sun, she doesn't care that it burns, he's pulling her head back by her hair and it's everything she's ever wanted.

"I'm going to make you come so hard. Don't disturb the neighbors," he whispered. She jumped and Vladimir hummed a low laugh.

"You know I've wanted to do this for so long."

"I know. You kept pushing it. Enough is enough."

Vladimir groaned, shoving his cock into the seam of her panties right between her lips and rubbed up against them.

"I can last a long time, woman."

"Well, what are you waiting for? Fuck me."

Vladimir moved the hand in her hair to her shoulder and he flipped her around again, roughly pulling her up off the table, moving her like a ragdoll to be in front of him. His lips are swollen and they haven't kissed yet.

"I think you need to do something for me first," he said.

Vladimir was going to make Natalia do his bidding just as much as she's going to make him do hers, and she can't wait to be bossed around and shoved in every direction possible. She hoped she emerges from the experience a changed woman, a woman of grace and dignity and her mile-wide dirty streak laid out bare for all her neighbors to hear, for the neighbor's sons one house over that like to watch her undress, she hopes they're all getting off to her getting fucked. She wanted the cops called and to fuck in front of them and then be handcuffed to Vladimir as they're shoved into the patrol car.

Vladimir's rough lips are on hers and she melted into them. It felt so wrong, but they were locked into position so well and Natalia was moaning in his mouth.

Vladimir pulled on her lip with his teeth and didn't let up when Natalia whined, stamping her foot and digging her nails into his arms. He bit down harder and Natalia knew the time for games with this young man was nearly over.

Chapter Four

It's so cold outside. Natalia wrapped her arms around Vladimir's shoulders feeling his sweat mingling with the sticky Corona residue. She scraped her nails across his back and he hissed.

The sun is going down, and Natalia's going to be in pain tomorrow but she'll like it. It would remind her of when she would get off to thinking about him in the morning when she took a shower. The steam bloomed up, the radio played loud and Natalia would scream, shoving her fingers into her mouth after making herself cum a few times.

"Oh," Vladimir sighed against her. "On your knees."

Before Natalia could react, he pulled her down by her hair, and she was buckling under his force not caring at all. She landed heavily in the grass on her knees and reached for his belt buckle in a split second, undoing it, yanking at it and popping his button-fly all the way down, six buttons too long.

When she pulled his jeans down to his thick thighs, she saw how hard this young man was, his cock bulging against his red boxers. There was a wet spot a mile wide where Vladimir's dripped for her, she wanted it in her mouth right now, so she could choke on him.

"Oh," Natalia moaned, making Vladimir moan, making his cock push up. She tucked fingers inside his briefs and rolled them down his hips and thighs.

His cock popped out and bounced in its weight. It's gigantic, Natalia noted as she splayed her fingers over the tip of it and dragged them down the length; long, uncut, and girthy, and Natalia felt herself aching with its absence inside of her.

Its foreskin was already sliding back, and Natalia tugged at it a little bit, pumped him around the base of the head and Vladimir bucked up and grunted, winding both of his hands into her hair and pulled a little. Natalia teased his skin over his head and back down, watching how it relaxed with her pull and tightened, just barely slipping over with her push, and he's dripping. It's going to slap Natalia's chest soon and she's going to put it between her breasts.

But she caught it with her tongue instead, the long string of pre-cum, and Vladimir moaned outright at the sight. She brought her tongue up to the head and circled around it, looking up at him with doe eyes while gripping him tightly.

Then, Natalia moved her hand to the base and she almost has her mouth around him, sucking a little but mostly getting used to the girth between her lips. Vladimir's moaning, wanting to set the pace but he's holding back, his fingers kept twitching forward before he can catch them.

Natalia took a deep breath, relaxed her throat, and then slid down, slipping him inside her mouth easily, her spit and his pre-cum are making it so easy to take it all in. She reached halfway and stopped, breathing around his cock for a moment.

"Hmm, can't do it, can you?" Vladimir gasped. He smirked, and she sucked harder, shutting him up momentarily with a moan.

"C'mon," he exhaled. "Take it. You want it, Natalia? Take it."

Natalia moaned before swallowing it all down, resting her sharp nose against his trimmed pubic hairs, breathing in slowly and going insane over his body odor.

"Yes," Vladimir sighed. "Just like that."

Natalia felt the wind blowing on the back of her neck and the little bit of her lower back exposed felt good.

Vladimir's fingers pulled her off him a little, then he shoved her back down and Natalia whimpered.

"I know," He said patronizingly, and she whimpered

again, shoving her free hand between her legs and rubbing up against it.

Vladimir fucked her face, slow at first, sliding himself almost all the way out of her mouth before giving her two small thrusts and then shoving himself all the way back in, and soon the older woman's choking on him. Her eyes were watering and she was about to cry, holding him at the base with her hand and not breathing, seeing stars and tightening up around his cock. Natalia's mouth was drooling, fully out of control, in his hands and he thrusting nonstop into her mouth.

"So...pretty...around my cock," he said gritting out.

She looked up seeing Vladimir's pupils are enlarged, his mouth is wide open and he's gasping, watching the way her lips drag against his cock when he pulls back.

"I'm about to—fuck—" Vladimir gasped and slipped out of her fast, and Natalia's gasped for air, gagging and coughing.

Vladimir's put his hands on her shoulders and bent over a little, panting and his eyes are clamped shut. Natalia wiped the drool off her mouth and chin and rubbed it into her thigh.

"Shit!"

Natalia didn't know what was hotter: Vladimir face-fucking her like she's always dreamed, or him trying so hard to hold back cumming.

Shortly, he raised up, a little more composed. He

pulled her up and brought her around to the long end of the table.

Vladimir pulled his top off over his head and Natalia's eyes darted to his abs flexing, making her mouth water more. When he leaned over Natalia to lay out his shirt on the table she pulled her own up and off, then her sports bra followed suit and Vladimir's laying those down too. He backed her up onto the table and Natalie straddled him rubbing her chest against his. Vladimir moaned with the feeling of her hardened nipples grazing his skin.

And the air is cool and wet against Natalie's skin, the dusk's light on her breasts as Vladimir kneaded them. He pinched her nipples and she yelped, kissing him, rubbing her tongue against his while Vladimir fiddles with the zipper of her shorts, pulling and unbuttoning them with one hand.

Vladimir then put his hand inside and Natalia moaned when he touched her wetness. He flicked around it before pulled her panties right up to rub over her clit.

"Ooooo! Ooooh!" She whined into his mouth. "Take them off, baby."

"No."

"Please, Vladimir," Natalie whispered, panting against his chin, kissing down his neck to his chest.

"Hmm, what did you say, baby?"

Natalia continued whining gripping at Vladimir's hips and ass. His jeans were still around his thighs, and Natalia shoved them down to his ankles, wrapped her legs around his and pinned his arm between them. “I would, but I don’t know how I can with you locking my arm.”

Natalia pushed herself off him faster than she can blink and Vladimir laughed. He took his hand out of her shorts and then yanked at them with both hands.

“Up,” he said.

It goes to Natalia’s core, she pushed herself on the table and her feet balanced on his strong calves, just enough for him to slide them off, and then Vladimir pulled them down making them dangle off her ankles for a second before falling onto the grass.

Vladimir took a step back and stared at Natalia, leaning back on her hands and panting. She’s so wet Vladimir can see her pussy stickiness. He then lunged back in and put his fingers inside of her. Natalia moaned, feeling slight burns but it felt so good. Just two of his fingers are stretching her pussy, but she wanted three, rather she wanted all of them and his cock in her at the same time.

“You’re so tight, Natalia,” Vladimir said. He slipped his fingers out almost all the way and then pushed them back in, twisting them around hitting a spot she swears no one else but herself has ever been able to do. “Oh, yeah? Right there, Fuck?” she yelled.

“Shush. The neighbors are going to hear us.”

“I don’t care. They watch me undress all the time.”

Vladimir chuckled as Natalia threw her head back, exposing her neck and chest to Vladimir's mouth. He ran his tongue flat up against her neck and sucked underneath her jawline as he worked her over with two fingers, digging deep inside of her and pulling up faster. He mixed up his pace and pattern and Natalia is soaking wet, completely undone by just two fingers.

"Right there," She panted. "Fuck—fuck—yes, Vlad."

"Yeah," He panted back. "Play with your clit."

Natalia sat up a little to reach down to her clit, it's was swollen and she jumped when she rubbed circles over it. Natalia's so wet and her pussy juice is everywhere; her fingers are slipping and sliding and she can't get good friction. Vladimir *laughs* at her, looking down and watching. His cock is rock hard and dripping onto her thigh and her hip and belly, bumping up against her sticky skin.

"Oh, having trouble?"

Natalia looked up and glared. He yanked her hand out of the way and replaced her fingers with his.

"I guess I have to do everything for you, Gaspazah," he said. Natalia moaned sitting back on her hands, watching him as he fingers her deep with one hand and played with her clit with the other. "Answer me."

"Yes, yes—daddy," she whined loud, and it embarrassed her.

"Yes, what did you say, Gaspazah?"

"Yes, Vlad. Oooo!—you have to do everything for me. I'm nothing without you."

Vladimir groaned and fingered her faster, pressing down harder on her clit and curling his fingers higher inside her.

He ruts against her as he worked her out, kissing her sloppily between pants and moans, and Natalia's stomach swooped low feeling her orgasm build more than she can ever recall.

"I'm going to come," Natalia whimpered, digging her nails into the table. "Oh my God! I'm going to come!"

"Yeah, give it to me," Vladimir said. "Come in my hand."

He flickered her clit faster. He's doing it just how she likes it, it's insanity, she's moving wildly.

Natalia gasped and Vladimir pulled his fingers up inside of her fast and repeatedly, fingering into her at the same speed and then Natalia screams his name and bears down on his fingers to dirty words of encouragement.

Vladimir didn't slow down. The tendons in his wrists are working overtime. Then, he eased up when Natalia jumped and he pulled his hands up, grabbing himself with one and her waist with the other.

"You look so good when you come."

Natalia didn't believe she's coming down from one of the biggest orgasms of her life. It's all from a man younger than her. She was screaming and moaning out loud in her backyard. It was all so surreal, and the alcohol and the chill outside wasn't helping her find her grasp on reality.

Vladimir then slid his cock against her pussy. Natalia's dripping and so is he, and he put it in with no problem.

"You don't wear condoms?"

"I don't have any."

"You're lucky I can't get pregnant."

Then, Vladimir's cock became tighter and Natalia hissed as Vladimir pulled out and then pushed back in to make some headway.

"It's so tight."

"I know Vladimir. It's been a few years since I've had sex," Natalia said.

"Lay back."

Natalia did and Vladimir slipped out, pushing her to scoot back until only her legs from the knees down are hanging off the side of the table. He climbed on top after kicking off boots and the remainder of his clothes.

He looked down at Natalia, splayed out underneath him, and smiled. For a moment, both of them snapped out of whatever sexy as fuck trance they were in, and laughed with each other.

Vladimir traced the side of Natalia's face.

"Wow," He sighed happily. "Took you long enough to say yes."

Natalia giggled and cuffed his shoulder lightly.

"Shut up."

"Hmm..." Vladimir raked his eyes up and down Natalia's body, sitting up on his knees and she can't stop staring at the short hairs on his thighs, his well-defined muscles and the way his hips are so strong and fit. His stomach's still a little soft, and God she loves it, she loves all of it.

Vladimir leaned back down and kissed her lifting one of her legs up over his shoulder.

"I'm going to fuck you so hard you're going to go blind," Vladimir said.

"Really?" Natalia moaned as Vladimir pushed inside of her.

His cock catches, but Vladimir pushes past it, pumping in and out of her in short bursts. Natalia relaxed feeling their wetness gliding him along. He bucked up in her, pushing all the way in and bottoming out and it *hurts.*

Natalia felt Vladimir push up against that spot again, the one just in front of her cervix and she's panting, digging her fingernails into his soft round ass.

She slapped it and Vladimir bucked into her, whining into her mouth, and she smacked it again, smoothing over his skin before smacking it a third time, and his whines matched hers in pitch and she laughed through their kisses.

His head dipped down and he's whining into her neck as she spanked him repeatedly, he's thrusting inside her roughly, barely pulling out at all, just hitting that spot over and over again.

"Come," he said. "Come, please, you're going to make me—"

"If I don't, what?"

"I will."

"Then come for your Gaspazah."

Natalia raised her other leg, slowly, to his head, and Vladimir groaned as his eyes caught it and watched her lower it onto his shoulder. Natalia's vagina opened completely for him, and Vladimir doubled down, pulling out further and pushing in harder.

It made Natalia hurt and ache and it was nothing like she ever felt before

"You're so big. Dammit!"

Vladimir's eyes rolled back at that and he groaned nodding. "So big that you're stabbing me."

"Oh, oh!" Vladimir panted.

"God I love it, it hurts, Vladimir, fuck, oh—"

"Oooo! Oooo! Gaspazah!"

He stroked faster, pushing harder and Natalia started thinking about how they were going to slide off the edge of this table any second.

"Natalia—" Vladimir dragged her name out on a long whine, he's fucking so fast she can't believe it, how strong this young man is, and how he hasn't given out yet.

"Oooo! Oh, Oh, Vladimir, I'm going to—"

Natalia doesn't finish her sentence before she came again, his cock's stroking just right, fast, hard and good.

Natalia's mouth is open but she isn't making any sounds, she isn't breathing, and Vladimir looked up at her and groaned as he watched her eyes roll back into her head. She grinned as she caught her breath and then she chanted out his name raggedly, over and over, and Vladimir's hips stuttered. He began cumming inside of her. "Oh, Gaspazah. Oh, Gaspazah!" Their juices dripped onto the table and both couldn't care less.

* * *

After a few moments, Vladimir slid out of her slowly groaning and rested on top of her. Natalia's legs were still up in the air over his shoulders as they laugh with the realization. Natalia unwinded herself from him as she sat up, pushing herself off the table.

Vladimir held her shoulders and kissed her, rubbing his thumbs against her cheek.

Natalia knows how fucked out she looks, her hair is everywhere and her lips are so swollen, they must look injected. Vladimir looked exhausted, sweaty, and was smiling.

"Are you done here, sir?"

"Yes, Gaspazah."

"Good. An forty-year-old plus woman like myself can only take a beating like this one in a while."

"Yes, Gaspazah."

"Go on, don't you have a date or something to go to?"

"I do."

"Well, hurry along. See you tomorrow when you come to finish this job of yours up."

"Ok, Gaspazah."

Mindy

Chapter One

It was a terrible evening for anyone to be out the Friday Eve of Valentine Day weekend. Rapidly falling temperatures with blustery winds had dominated the weather all day. As night came, freezing rain started falling making driving dangerous. Power was disrupted to most of the neighboring communities. This part of Alabama suffers bad weather from many fronts; ice storms, hurricanes, and tornados. This early-February storm was a bad one.

As the store manager for a prominent grocery chain, I needed to balance the emergency supply needs of our customers and safety of my associates. Early shoppers were heeding storm predictions with practiced preparations, stocking up on water, dry ice, batteries, and food. Many local businesses sent their employees home midday, creating a large afternoon surge of customers at my store.

The greater than normal shopper numbers and product demands required adjustments by my store's personnel. We instituted our storm operation plan that changes task priorities. Several department managers called in extra help. With a similarly practiced preparation, my store smoothly moved customers and product out the doors.

When the shopper volume started slacking off, I began sending some associates home. The teenage minors were first despite only working a few hours since arriving after school. Associates that had longer distances to go or feared driving in the worsening conditions followed. While we still had enough workers, we buttoned up the bakery, meat, and produce departments; they had little traffic anyway. The deli manager kept two sandwich makers until the rotisserie and fryer were empty. The pharmacist stayed as long as we remained open to run the pharmacy alone.

By the time the rains came, customer traffic had dwindled to a few stragglers. I was running the front end of the store with one cashier, a department manager running the customer service desk, and two stockers. We were all middle-aged or older men with short distances to travel home so we hung on to be there for the community.

The store lights went out when our area's power went

down, coming back on immediately as our generator kicked in. Corporate equips all stores with generators capable of running entire chains for at least 72 hours.

In response to the power blip, I stepped out from the money-room to see the store still lit and one of our cashiers scanning a customer's purchase. Walking over to look out the front doors, I saw we had the only lights in the neighborhood. The wind was howling and blowing the rain sideways; sleet covered one side of a nearby fire-lane sign. I saw only one car slowly moving along on the highway and decided to close the store as soon as possible.

* * *

I turned to see three customers lined up at the single aisle so I made my way to the manager's register. I called over the last customer in line as I was having trouble logging in. By the time I got to the customer, her back was to me while she put her things onto the conveyor. She had on a black hostess uniform and her legs were bare. Raindrop circles peppered her blouse's sleeves and her hair was mildly wet. She appeared to be quite young, causing me to worry for her experience driving in the storm.

Focused on scanning her purchases and putting them in bags, I never looked up at her. Even when I scanned the wine she purchased and asked for her identification, I looked at her hand to grasp her license. My eyes went straight to the date-of-birth field; she was twenty-four. When I held out her license, she didn't take it back, leaving me to scan her groceries one-handed. After a few seconds, I looked up.

"Don't you remember me, Freddie?"

How could I forget Mindy Myers? This young lady had grown up since I saw her last. She was a small-breasted, average-looking naive girl and despite her plainness, something exciting about her presence awakened my desire this evening.

Oh, Mindy still favors that red lipstick; her pale Nicole-Kidman-looking skin made her appearance a stunning geisha-like contrast.

Tipping her right hip up, Mindy put her hand on her waist and poked out her lips. Then she closed her eyes and stuck out her tongue. *My God! This young woman hasn't learned, yet.* When Mindy opened her eyes, she caught me staring. I knew she was teasing me but in a peevish-tart persona. *Little did I know that it would be more than just that.*

Chapter Two

A little background on Mindy Myers

Mindy was an amateur actress who could make anyone laugh with her character improvisations. I have personally seen her speak as a bookish nerd, a drippy-sweet southern belle, and a fast-talking, gum-smacking, valley girl at a few town events. Her talents impressed me back when she was a freshman in junior high school. She was always involved in school plays and theater and had a decent singing voice. Her plans for a career in show business were a foregone conclusion when I last saw her.

Mindy started her first job as a part-time summer hire at a store in Florida where I was sent as the assistant store manager a few years ago. She worked with us for a little over two years until she left for college.

* * *

Friendly and vivacious, Mindy hugged everyone she had liked. After hugging me the first time, I had to advise her to avoid hugging managers or supervisors, and warned her to avoid displays of affection with her peers in front of customers. She was smart and mature for her age, understanding my advice was direction about social propriety in the workplace and not criticism of her nature. Mindy broke the no-hugging rule one time in her last summer of work when she expressed her condolences after I lost my wife to breast cancer. *Of course, I paid it no mind.*

Moreover, Mindy had a habit of sticking out her tongue at people. To be fair, sticking out a tongue appeared to be a greeting behavior many minors from her Florida high school practiced were doing to some degree. She did it to me a few times until I told her, "When I was a teenager, sticking out your tongue was an invitation to be kissed. Whatever it means to you, I think you should not do that at the workplace." She stopped doing it to me, at least. Tonight, she appeared to reprise the action deliberately.

* * *

Back to the present

My thoughts wavered as I was trying to grasp whether Mindy was teasing me or signaling that she wanted me to kiss her. Her lips parted again to show her tongue that seemed to beckon me.

I managed to respond to her in a business-like manner. "Of course, I remember you, young lady."

She looked bemused and slowly shook her head. Responding using her southern belle accent, Mindy mildly complained. "Y'all always maintained proper decorum, bless your heart. But sweetie, I'm an adult now and since I don't work here no more, I wish you'd address me less formally, Freddie."

I paused to look into her brown eyes. Her eyebrows lifted. Caught off-guard by her flirtatious demeanor, I responded, "Of course, Mindy. You are right."

Her shoulders drooped as she began to rummage in her purse. Then, she looked up at me again. "Forgive me if I've been insensitive, Mr. Fred. Are you still mourning Jill's passing?"

"Mindy, you are anything but insensitive. Jill was the best part of my life for a long time and I will remember her forever but I have moved on. This weather situation has me as well as everyone stressed. I should apologize for acting so business-like. Hug me, Mindy."

She yipped and moved toward the end of the register. I came around from my side to meet her with open arms. The back of her clothing was wetter than I imagined and her hug was more intense than the embraces I felt from her before.

More than just putting her arms around me, Mindy's chest pushed firmly against mine as her hips and thighs were making contact with me as well. Although I felt a twinge of arousal, I don't think Mindy was coming on to me. However, her position demonstrated an adult level of affection.

She held me tight and the hug lasted for several seconds. I could not help enjoying the feeling of holding her in my arms. Not wanting the hug to end, I waited for her to pull away first. When she did, I murmured into her ear, "It's nice to see you again, Mindy," and pecked her cheek lightly.

As her arms released, my hand rose to touch her cheek where I had kissed her. She gazed at me for a moment with her mouth open. Seconds later, she whispered, "Does that mean I can kiss you now, daddy?"

I couldn't deny the chance of kissing this young woman was a delightful prospect to me. My position at the store precluded such an exchange with a customer would be improper. I then gave her a veiled promise, "Not here, my dear."

Mindy nodded and backed away, speaking wistfully to herself. "There you go, Mindy. You have something to look forward to now." While waiting for her credit card in the reader to be processed, Mindy wrote her cellphone number on the back of a piece of one of our sales papers. "So we can meet elsewhere when you are less busy, daddy." She putting her hand on her chest and patted herself briefly. "Whew! Be still heart of mine."

Admittedly pursuing a relationship with a woman less than half my age was something very much out of our small town's conservative norms. Yet, stranger things have happened here as well.

Chapter Three

When I finished processing Mindy's purchase, I walked her to the door. The winds that drove the rain horizontal made the weather colder as we stepped outside. I suggested to Mindy to leave her buggy with me while she brought her car to the front entrance.

After reaching her car, Mindy managed to edge it slipping and sliding to a halt at the front entrance. I had her stay in the car while I placed her bags in the backseat. She told me that her apartment was only a few miles away, so I told her to drive as slow as possible. I watched as her car struggled to climb the slight incline out of the parking lot onto the highway.

* * *

Once Mindy was out of sight, I hurried inside, making an announcement on the PA system that the store was now closing. I was the last to leave the store nearly thirty minutes after everyone else and the weather had indeed gotten worse.

The parking lot challenged my work boots as I made it finally to my car. I spent several minutes scraping the ice from the windows, my hands and cheeks stinging. After warming up for a minute or two, I began my commute home.

* * *

Seeing several abandoned vehicles along the highway, I was relieved to find that none of them matched Mindy's. Following my normal route, a mile down the highway, I turned down a two-lane road. In the darkness, I could not see ice on the road but I could feel it was there. Driving under twenty miles-per-hour, my vehicle occasionally spun its wheels going up small hills and slipped sideways. Once I reached the hill's peak, I saw trouble at the bottom. There were hazard lights flashing from a car ahead amongst the bushes down an embankment; someone was standing at the edge of the road.

Still, a hundred yards away from the person standing there, I saw the person trying to flag me down. I recognized from the clothing that it was Mindy. When I got closer, my headlights began illuminating her bigger and bigger. Mindy started running gingerly in my direction on the icy grass, trying not to slip down the embankment.

When she reached my door, I pushed it open from the inside. "Get in," I said.

Mindy climbed in quickly, "Thank you for s-st... Freddie! Thank God, you c-came. I thought I was going to f-freeze to death," Mindy stuttered.

She was shivering, whimpering, her teeth were chattering making it difficult for her to speak. I turned the heater on high and adjusted the vents to blow directly on her. I took off my jacket and gave it to her to use as a blanket.

* * *

From our brief conversation, I learned what steps Mindy had taken to affect rescue. Both local and county police units were swamped with calls and were experiencing difficulties getting around, the dispatcher advised her to wait in her car. Mindy also called Triple-A and similarly, the agent advised her that the chance of a tow truck responding anytime soon was unlikely.

Mindy tried moving her car herself but discovered she had no traction in the mud, risking sliding further down into a creek, just yards away.

She decided to stand at the side of the road, falling twice trying to climb the embankment before she got to an area of bushes and saplings she could use to pull herself up. Fifteen minutes later, I was the first car to come upon her.

* * *

Mindy called 911 again to report I was there to give her a ride so they could take her off their rescue list. Next, I suggested that she cancel the request for towing assistance until after the storm.

I took Mindy's keys and grabbed a flashlight from the glove compartment to go out and check on her vehicle.

When I took my first step on the ground, I fell flat on my back and slid like a human toboggan into a puddle at the bottom of the embankment. I eventually made it to her car and shut off her hazard flashers. I then grabbed her groceries; four plastic bags and started heading back up the embankment. Holding the flashlight while slipping and sliding in the dark also complicated my climb back up.

I fell three more times. Without a free hand, I couldn't use the bushes and saplings as Mindy had done. I ended up threading my way almost fifty yards to where the embankment was negligible. By the time I reached my SUV wet and muddy, I was freezing, near the levels of hypothermia Mindy was experiencing.

* * *

Driving at a snail's pace, I worried about Mindy getting warm. We talk about how the power outage in her area was worse than mine. She didn't even know what kind of heating system she had in her unit. I chuckled that Mindy was still learning the ropes.

My house was about two miles closer than Mindy's place. When I suggested going to my place until the storm died down, Mindy agreed that was a great idea.

Chapter Four

Mindy was shivering so badly, she could hardly climb out of my SUV and stumbled as she walked. Holding her with my arm around her shoulders and using my flashlight to light our way, I led Mindy straight to my master bathroom.

"Let's get you a hot shower right away," I said.

Mindy started undressing. I propped up the flashlight to shine on the ceiling. Reaching into the shower stall, I turned on the water for her.

Anxious to warm up, Mindy hadn't waited for me to leave the room to finish taking off her things. When I turned from the shower stall, she was unbuttoning the last button on her blouse. She didn't seem to care if I was looking. Before I even took a step, she had yanked her blouse off, showing off her black lacy bra. I saw the dark areolae through the bra's wet fabric. As I stepped past her, she was reaching behind her back to unhook her bra, her smallish breasts came outward.

The only towel in the bathroom was one I used that morning and hung up. "I'll get a fresh towel for you. I have a bathrobe you can use, too." In her haste to get under the hot water, Mindy only gave a terse acknowledgment.

Mindy was facing two mirrors over my jetted tub in the corner adjacent to the shower stall. The mirrors' positions gave me a triple bank, frontal view of Mindy getting naked as we chatted. I should have looked away but was mesmerized as Mindy slid's skirt and panties fell on the ground revealing her bush. I quickly left the room as Mindy stepped into the shower.

* * *

Using my cellphone's torch, I found my flashlight and lantern and put them in the bathroom. Then, I got the fireplace started after I swung a sofa around to face it. Afterward, I threw a few pillows and comforter on the sofa along with a bedsheet. Finally, I lit some candles and turned on the radio.

* * *

Minutes later, I headed back to the bathroom with a fresh towel and red silky robe that I got from Japan for my late wife on one of our vacations. I loved when she wore it and refused to part with it. I now didn't mind if Mindy wore it.

The bathroom door was cracked open and the shower was running. I knocked then spoke through the crack, "I'm bringing in a towel and robe."

"Okay, Freddie."

I entered and set up the lantern on the vanity, kept my face turned away but my urges led me to take sneak peeks. Mindy was rinsing her hair with her back to the spray, I could see her open eyes and I knew she could see me close by, looking at her through the glass.

My gaze first focused on her ruby lips, then dropped down to her areolae, before locking onto the dark triangle of her young bush. I started getting hard but doubted she'd noticed.

"Are you going to shower now?" Mindy asked.

"When you're done."

"You don't have to wait, Daddy."

"Mindy, just save me some hot water." My cock was rock hard. I left the bathroom quickly embarrassed about bailing out on the golden opportunity.

* * *

I set out my robe and boxers on the bed, then went to

stand in front of the fireplace. I was trembling, excited about what may lie ahead with this young lady.

"This robe's really nice. I love its silky feeling," Mindy said as she entered the living room. "It was Jill's, wasn't it? I should take it off—"

"No, please don't. Jill was such a sharing person she would have given you anything of hers. She also made me promise to get on with my life and never let memories of her hold me back from life without her. The fact that I kept her bathrobe of all things suggests destiny meant for you to wear it tonight. You look great in red, you know. The robe matches your favorite color of lipstick."

My comment made Mindy detour to her purse to apply a fresh coat to her lips, continuing my opportunity to observe from all angles how the robe looked on her. The silk's sheen shimmered in the candlelight; in front of the fire making a dancing golden glow.

Mindy entered the room walking toward me, the mid-thigh length robe clinging to her jiggling breasts and tips of her nipples. The robe's petite size on Mindy's taller frame barely covered her torso, exposing the entirety of her youthful legs.

She bent over to reach in her purse on my low-end table, the hem of the robe rose up in the back but I was too close behind her to see anything. While Mindy put on her lipstick, I went back to the fire and waited for her to bend over again. I had a brief view of her naked cheeks, but alas, I only saw shadows in the dim light. Somehow, the hint of her private area was more erotic than blatant exposure.

* * *

I wasn't used to this much visual stimulation. Mindy's display turned me on. It was dawning on me that perhaps she was putting on a show. She knew I would watch her staged entrance. Bending over like that and her shower exposure was just the beginning of her deliberate actions. My hunch was confirmed when I saw Mindy look for a bulge in my pants. She smiled seeing it but said nothing.

I needed to get out of my wet clothes and into a hot shower. I ushered Mindy in front of the fireplace, told her to make herself comfortable and find some music she liked on the radio if she wished. I told her I'd be back out in a few minutes.

* * *

Standing in the shower with my eyes closed, the hot water relaxed me. I had been enjoying the spray only about thirty seconds when Mindy's voice in the bathroom startled me.

"Do you have a hairbrush I can use?"

I turned instinctively to hide my nakedness even as

my eyes opened to see the fuzzy image of her head leaning in from the doorway, looking in my direction.

"In the middle drawer," I answered.

Watching her over my shoulder, I saw that she kept her head turned toward me as she walked inside. My body turned slightly to allow my eyes to follow her. Retracing her steps, Mindy was looking at me again, wanting to see my cock I imagined. Her boldness excited me. Remaining motionless even when as she reached the doorway and paused, I let her have another sideways look she obviously wanted to get. The thrill of exposure made my heart pound ... and then she was gone.The blood flow that filled my cock was rushing; Mindy was exciting me in ways I had never experienced before. I stroked myself to full hardness as images of Mindy in my late wife's red robe and me naked in front of her just moments ago danced in my head. I was sure I was going to have sex. Still, I contemplated masturbating to ensure I wouldn't come prematurely with her. Then, the water temperature started dropping, so I hurried to finish my shower.

* * *

I had just buried my face in my towel to dry off when Mindy's voice made me jump again. "I found your wine glasses but not a corkscrew. Do you have one?"

I lowered my arms to drape my towel in front of me as

I looked over my shoulder at her. She had stepped boldly through the doorway to stand behind me instead of asking from the other side.

"There should be one in the drawer under the microwave."

Instead of heading off, Mindy remained there looking at my bare back and then asked, "Aren't you going to finish drying yourself?"

I started moving the towel around my arms and chest while protecting my modesty. Mindy stood watching but soon grew impatient. "Aren't you going to dry your back?" I shrugged, so she asked, "Afraid I'll see something? Daddy, you're already showing me what a cute butt you have."

I reacted without thinking, grabbing the lower edge of the towel and pulling it over my ass. She suddenly looked past me; her eyes grew large and twinkled. "Oh, that's even cuter," she chirped and then left the bathroom giggling. My head spun around to see myself in the mirror, looking like a matador pulling my cape out of the way of my charging cock. At least, she saw me hanging heavy and not shriveled.

* * *

When I entered my bedroom to dress, I noticed my boxers on my bed were gone. Mindy moved them, presumably so I would be naked under my robe. T*his young lady wants me or am I going crazy?*

I walked into the living room seeing that Mindy had moved the sofa cushions onto the floor and covered them with the sheet. She was sitting in the lotus position facing the fire. She had opened the wine and set out a glass for each of us on the edge of the hearth.

Walking up beside her, I caught a brief glimpse of her hairy slit as she adjusted herself to make room for me. I put my arm around her and pulled her close, picking up the wine glass and offered a toast. "To your rescue."

She countered, "To my hero." We clinked glasses and took long sips.

Chapter Five

Having decided the time was right to respond to Mindy's overtures, I wanted to lean in to kiss her but she was staring into the fire. I waited while she remained introspective, sensing she might be concerned about us. We were half way through our second glass before I decided to end the prolonged silence. "Are you all right, Mindy? You seem troubled by something."

She turned her head to look at me "I am, Freddie. I fear I may have been out of line tonight. I called you a *hero* because you certainly are that for saving my life tonight but you're more than that to me. I've always been fond of the way you treat other people, especially the teenagers at the store. You have a mature sense I wish I could find in young guys. I know you're older but when I learned tonight that you're still unattached, I figured to catch your eye somehow. Then it seemed I had a perfect opportunity to be intimate with you but you've showed little interest. I guess I'm too young for you or you don't like young ladies coming onto you. I'm sorry for how I've acted."

"No need to apologize. You're neither too young nor too aggressive. I am interested in you beyond the ways we used to interact as coworkers. You are such a talented person with a wonderful personality that has always made me take notice. Today, I felt some conflicts about when I could respond to you but they weren't about if I should. The only thing about our age difference that I worry about is whether I would be judged as taking advantage of you. Yet, we are two single adults free to follow our desires wherever they take us."

As I was speaking, her facial expression slowly changed to a smile. I stuck out my tongue and she reacted immediately, turning her shoulders to bring her lips to my mouth. As forward as she acted about showing affection, I expected her to kiss me passionately.

Instead of wet and energetic, Mindy's kiss was soft and warm. Her tongue was gentle and encouraging instead of aggressive and self-serving. She was showing me she had deep feelings for me rather than just following an impulse to have a carefree romp in bed. Yet, the prospect of sex was arousing me underneath.

Mindy pulled back from our kiss and opened her eyes.

"Darlin', I love the way you kiss me," she cooed. "I like soft ones with a skillful tongue. You made me tingle down to my toes."

I looked down into the space between us. Mindy's robe sash had loosened during our kiss and my hand at her waist holding her close to me was all that held her robe closed. I pulled my hand away. In the gap between slack lapels, I saw the soft side of her breast and a small patch of her cunt hair. I looked at her again while my hand pulled her robe completely open. Mindy's eyes widened and her mouth opened.

I gently cupped her breast, rubbing her thick and long nipple of her smallish mound. Mindy's eyes closed, her head lolled back, as she exhaled. "Ahhh. Your touch is so gentle, Freddie."

I played with her nub then pulled her in for another long kiss. Mindy pushed her breast against my caresses and moaned. Her breathing through her nose began to hiss with excitement.

Years of abstinence and Mindy's responding, youthful body made my cock hard as a stone; I didn't know if I would make to the bed without coming on myself. I tried to ignore sensations but failed when Mindy upped the ante.

Mindy's hand dropped to my thigh. The warmth of her hand and softness of her fingers on my flesh left me breathless. Then she started moving up my leg and under my robe. My precum was increasing as Mindy curled her fingers around it.

"Whoa! Somebody is excited," she said, then added matter-of-factly, "So am I."

Mindy held my cock as I untied my sash and pulled my robe open. Our lips were in contact again as I leaned against her, guiding her backwards until we were prone on the cushions. I came down next to her, her arm trapped under me still holding and tugging my cock. We then restarted momentarily but I had other plans. I started sucking on her nipple while my other hand went into her dense bush.

Mindy's legs spread for me, offering me unhindered access to her vulva. Sliding through loose labial folds, I slipped my fingers into her vagina, coating them with her copious wetness before pulling them back along her slit. She let out a soft sigh when I touched her clit. As my finger teased her, her hips began to squirm. I hadn't been fingering her very long when she startled me by saying, "You're starting to leak. Are you about to come?"

"It's been years since I've been intimate with a woman. I probably won't be able to last long."

"Then let's make our first time all about you, Daddy. Enter me now and we'll celebrate a new start for you, something I really want to be a part of. Besides, I come very easily. Maybe I'll surprise you or you'll last longer than you think."

* * *

I rose to my knees, Mindy still was holding onto my cock. Her knees folded and her legs swung out of my way as she guided me around in front of her. I looked down at her pubes creating a dark Fu Manchu around her pink gash, a stark contrast to her thighs and tummy. Her inner labia pulled open as her legs lifted and spread just before she guided me in. Leaning, I watched my cock disappear. Her vagina was snug but pliant and well lubricated, allowing me to slide in easily, as if sucked in.

I paused fully inserted, "Oh, Lord!" I moaned. *What a feeling to be inside a woman again*! Mindy sighed softly with me. Her arms reached up to pull me down to her so she could kiss me. Her legs were around my waist, ankles hooked behind my butt. Mindy had me locked and loaded, my cock buried in her heavenly wetness.

I was afraid to thrust at a fast pace, certain that I would come too quickly. Surging forward and downward, I slowly but forcefully drove myself deep until my hips pushed against Mindy's body. As I began repeating the rhythm, Mindy grunted with each thrust and emitted little mews.

"Fuck, Daddy! You're so huge..." Mindy moaned.

I wish she'd stop moaning because I was so close.

The rhythm of our undulations slowly sped up. With my hands under her shoulders, my elbows at her sides supported most of my upper body weight. Our increasing level of exertion and excitement were gasps in lungfuls of air. Slapping and squishing noises from us colliding became intense accents to our act of sex.

"Oh, Freddie!" caused me to direct my attention to see Mindy's rapturous facial expressions. I was trying so hard to avoid coming early but now settled in to concentrate on Mindy's reactions to our copulation; I did what I could to increase her pleasure first. The result was a dramatic shift in my performance and prolonged endurance.

Her hands slid down my back to grab my butt cheeks and as she began forcefully urging me into her. Instead of holding back, I began to pounding my cock into her. I marveled how my impacts jerked Mindy's body, causing her legs to wave in the air, and making her breasts shake like mounds of Jell-O. My resurgence continued to escalate Mindy's bliss. Her soft noises became squeals. Her hips rolled her pussy to receive every plunge eagerly.

"Oh, Freddie, oh Freddie! Fuck me..."

As I continued to slam into her, Mindy became increasingly vocal, calling out my name, expressing her joy, and praising my penetrations. These were reactions I had never witnessed from my wife or my limited number of previous lovers. Combined with Mindy body's intense physical arousal, I was having a sexual experience unlike any before.

Encouraged on by Mindy's pleasure, I channeled my

efforts to push her over the edge. And she made it obvious when I succeeded. Shrieking my name repeatedly: *Freddie, Freddie,* her hands clutched and clawed on my back; her legs clamped like a vise around my waist; her vagina clamped down on my cock. A gush of Mindy's vaginal fluids soaked my cock and ran down my legs, warming my skin and filling my nostrils with her womanly scent.

"Sheesh, you're running like the Niagara River, sweetheart," I said as her convulsions diminished. Proudly, I felt encouraged to continue and give this young woman another thorough pounding.

"Oh, Freddie! You're wonderful," Mindy panted, her breathing nearly returned to normal.

***

Mindy's ankles were unhooked, her legs fell down beside my hips as I pushed myself up. Looking down at my cream-coated shaft bridging the gap between our soaked pubes, I made sure the head of my cock stayed inside her as I adjusted our position. I lifted her by the hips and rose to a kneeling position. I then shifted to one side and levered her opposite leg up onto my shoulder. Leaning to the other side, I brought her second leg up.

Mindy's heels were pressed against my ears as I leaned downward, bending her in half. My cock slid deep into her until my pubic bone mashed against her clit.

Mindy let out a whiny groan, *Fuck* and opened her eyes to stare into mine hovering inches above her.

Leaning my torso down further while keeping my head above hers, my cock provided a balancing fulcrum allowing me to hold my legs suspended in the air. With most of my weight pressing on her hips, I sqquirmed and rocked my body to drill into her pussy. Her open eyes widened and she gasped, "Oh! Oh! Oh!"

My toes touched down, I bent at the waist enough to withdraw partially, and then kicked my legs airborne again as I drove harder down into her. Mindy reacted, surprised by the force of my entry. I began repeating the maneuver as if hopping into her vagina like a pogo stick, eliciting another episode of vocal responses from Mindy.

I found a sexual power I never knew I possessed. My engorged cock felt unstoppably solid as I rammed into her until I felt her convulsions starting again after only a dozen or so thrusts. This time, her orgasm triggered mine. Satisfied that I had performed my best, I let my come rage.

"Yes, Freddie. Yes, give it to me—" Mindy moaned into my ear.

I felt Mindy's convulsions pulling spurt after spurt of cum from my cock in the most pleasurable orgasm I could remember having. I was growling as I rocked with ecstasy; Mindy was squealing and thrashing under me.

"Oh, fuck Mindy! Fuck!" I panted.

What seemed like minutes of sexual bliss, reality

slowly regained focus. We were panting, covered with mixed sexual excretions and perspiration. I looked down Mindy's chest. Her eyes were on me with a dreamy gaze.

* * *

Mindy's hand came up to caress my cheek, whispering as she spoke, "Freddie, you rocked my world. I've never had sex this good before." Her body was still shivering.

I honestly believed my sexual prowess was underdeveloped after having only a few previous partners and a comparatively bland marital sex-life. *Mindy was of a different generation of sexual freedom; a hookup culture that was not existent in my days. The men in my generation often had to wait months and sometimes years before getting lucky. This thing with Mindy happened all in one night, my God!*

I responded, "Honey, I've never had better sex either. I never had a partner react to my lovemaking like you just did. Yeah, not even Jill. You inspired me to try new things and focus on your pleasure more than my own. You made me the lover I was tonight."

"You were unbelievable, Freddie. I can't believe how things worked out. I've wanted to be with you for a long time. Now that I am, I want to be with you forever."

"What did she just say?" I thought, *"Aren't we moving just a little too fast?"*

Mindy's eyelids fluttered and body shivered again. This time, her vaginal spasm pushed my cock out. I shifted my body off hers and we laid side-by-side.

For about thirty minutes, we cuddled, kissed, and talked. We were connecting on an emotional level as deeply as the passion had united our bodies.

Chapter Six

Mindy rolled onto her back to reach for her wine glass on the hearth but stopped in mid-reach. She uttered, "Uh oh!" and shifted her butt to expose a large puddle of fluids where she had been lying. "We made a mess on the sheets and should change them before it soaks through to your cushions."

Mindy stood up, put her hand between her legs. "There's a lot more of you and me coming out. I'm going to shower again, dear."

"Ok, love."

Meanwhile, Mindy waddled off toward the bathroom with a hand still between her legs. *Oh shit! I forgot to use a condom. What if she's pregnant?* I thought grabbing the sheets to drop in the washer while I was close behind her. I was anxious to get the hot water going, but Mindy stepped into the shower stall first.

I caught up, noticing Mindy looking at her cum-smeared hand and struggling to remove her robe one-handed. As quick as I could, I pulled it off her shoulders, hung hers and mine on the hooks, and then stepped into the stall with her. Turning the showerhead, I let the water flow until it was hot.

* * *

Once the water was cascading on us, I pulled her close and kissed her deeply. Her young lips were soft and sensuous as before yet suggestive of a hunger for more passion. The way her body pressed against me defined our new intimacy. Mindy's soft breasts pressed against me and pubic hairs tickled my dangling cock until my excitement awakened.

Mindy looked down at it after our kiss ended. A devilish smile curled her lips before she knelt in front of me. With her face inches away, Mindy grabbed my cock and balls.

"This is one big boy!"

One hand curled around my cock as it stroked up and down my shaft, the other rubbed and kneaded my balls as I moaned. Without soap, Mindy scrubbed me clean and the stimulating effect gave me an erection for the ages.

When she stopped washing it off, she held it pointed at her face; her eyes focused on it as if she was inspecting her work.

After several seconds, Mindy looked up at me and said, "You look good enough to eat, daddy!"

I hate to admit, I've never had a real blowjob before. My wife Jill had too much aversion to it, never making more than a few half-hearted attempts to please me. She felt the same about me going down on her. Let's just say that she was old-school.

I wanted to experience this so badly. I stood up straight as this woman looked eager to fulfill my wildest dreams. She seemed to hesitate for a few moments until her mouth suddenly opened and her tongue flitted across her upper lip. Leaning her head closer, Mindy reached out to lick over my cock. I could hardly breathe.

Mindy plunged me deeply into her mouth so suddenly, I gasped. "Oh fuck, Mindy!" Her head bobbed forcefully several times, taking as much of me as would fit. Then she mouthed me in a circular fashion. There were incredible sensations from her tongue, lips, and breath all at once devouring me.

"Fuck, Mindy! Fuck!" I panted leaning my head and shoulders back against the wall. I lightly held her head with my hands to feel its motion, and closed my eyes to focus. Mindy was doing everything she could to make me come, seemingly ready to take it in her mouth. I hoped to do that very thing but I would give her a warning.

Her hands grabbed my buttocks and pulled me forward as her lips slid all the way to my cock's base. Its head had to be pushing down her throat yet she held me there for seconds at a time. It felt as if she was trying to milk the semen from my balls, my senses were so focused on her that the background noise of the shower faded from my consciousness. As Mindy sucked more and more, I heard her breathy noises and squishy sounds of saliva overtake the sounds of the shower.

"Oh, fuck! It feels so good..." I moaned feeling a fiery tingle building, I wanted to hold back, to feel it longer. Every muscle in my body tensed; I rose on my toes; my mouth gaped open but no air entered. I lost control, giving her no more warning than a guttural cry as I erupted.

"Fucccckkkkkk!" I slurred elongating every letter. It was the best I can do as I rocked left and right.

Mindy accepted each of my spurts with a happy *'mmm-hmm'* sound. Her throat noises confirmed she was swallowing every drop until my orgasm was over.

Chapter Seven

I leaned against the wall in hazy, post-orgasm awareness when Mindy stood up. Her face seemed to rise out of a cloud of steam and meet with mine for a long kiss. After it ended, I realized that we were probably swapping cum but I tasted nothing and wasn't bothered by the thought.

I continued watching as Mindy started washing her pussy, I wanted to do for her as she did me. By the time I got it together, my mental stupor rinsed away right around the same time the water temperature began dropping. Mindy finished up and turned off the shower.

We dried off and I was thinking that I needed at least an hour to get hard again. I was surprised how fast Mindy made me come.

* * *

After putting on our robes in the bathroom, we scurried through cool spaces of the house to the warmth in front of the fireplace. I sat down first and poured another glass of wine for each of us while Mindy stood nearby brushing her hair. Her raised arms held her robe wide open, catching my attention when I noticed her cunt exposed. I took advantage to examine every intimate detail of her vulva with unabashed interest.

When Mindy noticed me staring, she stepped closer and straddled my legs, shamelessly displaying her flesh just inches from my face. The suggestive offer for oral sex clearly signaled what she wanted me to do. I was afraid I would be clumsy and demonstrate my lack of cunnilingus experience but went forth with it.

My hand rose to push fingers into her loosely hanging labia. Mindy stopped brushing her hair, letting her arms hang at her sides. She began to squirm as I explored her warm folds and then slipped my fingers into her. Cum quickly oozed over my hand and her heady musk gave my cock new life.

"Yes, Daddy! You like your girl, don't you?" Mindy moaned when I grabbed her butt and pulled her forward against my face. The hairbrush clattered on the floor as my nose burrowed deeply in her pubes. My mouth pushed between her labia and my tongue was on her swollen clit. The taste and aroma of Mindy was an aphrodisiac, filling me with an animalistic desire I haven't had ever. Tasting her young twat brought my fifth sense into play, enhancing my initiation into orally pleasing a woman.

I could tell Mindy's pleasure was most intense when my tongue danced on her clit, so I concentrated my efforts there. Using my fingers to spread her labia and lift her clit's hood created additional visual opportunities to witness her arousal in detail from a vantage point I never experienced. Hearing her moans and groans were not new but the intensity fluctuations gave me encouraging feedback for my newfound skillset.

"I need to lie down before you make me pass out."

I helped her turn and fall gently backward onto the cushions. She spread her legs, eagerly opening her gash for my tongue. From pushing my tongue as far into her vagina as it could reach to licking and nipping her clit with my teeth, I ravaged her.

"Oh, Daddy! You're...fucking—" Mindy moaned unable to complete her sentence.

Meanwhile, I felt unhurried to bring her to orgasm, wanting the heavenly feast to last as long as possible, yet within a minute or two she came so much for me. Her vaginal secretions flowed onto my face; her hands held my head firmly against her bucking hips; and her whines became shrieks. "Yikes, Daddy! Ah, ah, Oh my God!"

I looked up to watch Mindy's blissful facial expressions as I was a spectator to her climax. Instead, I kept up urgent stimulations through waves of convulsions until like reins on a horse, her hands in my hair slowed us to a stop.

Listening to her gasping breaths and feeling her body quiver repeatedly, I held my lips around her clit. Impulsively, my tongue gave her love-nub a poke causing her to jerk spasmodically. When I did it again, Mindy moaned loudly and she grasped onto my hair. I wasn't sure of her reactions, so I lifted my head. Immediately, her hands pushed my face back down.

"Eat me, Daddy! Don't stop..."

I was thrilled to oblige. I brought Mindy to three more strong orgasms until her hands pulled me off her. Pulling my head to guide me up to hers, Mindy deeply kissed me, her mouth was coated with her juices.

"Daddy', you are such an awesome lover. I can't believe how lucky I am to be with you." I felt her hand rubbing my cock. "If this means you've got something left to give, I want you to put it in me again, Freddie."

I rose on my knees and plunge it inside her without resistance.

"Aye!" Mindy moaned. Her vagina was so hot, wet, and loose that I was sliding in and out of her easily. Soon, she was begging me to fuck her harder. I pounded away with surprising stamina.

Amid moans and cries, Mindy spoke in a nearly delirious babble as her passion blossomed one more time. I cried out her name and erupted inside her just minutes later. Because of the narrowness of the sofa cushions, Mindy rolled onto her side, and we spooned quietly, facing the fire.

I draped my arm over her side and cupped her breast. Her hand covered mine and our fingers entwined. I kissed the back of her neck and said, "Goodnight, Mindy." Giving my hand a squeeze, she responded in kind.

As the veil of sleep crept over me, I heard her whisper, "I love you, Freddie."

Was I dreaming or did Mindy actually say that?

Chapter Eight

I woke up from a strange dream of me walking in a park with Mindy who was pushing a baby stroller. I thought again about me not wearing a condom.

Looking around, I realized the light coming from my bathroom was brighter than the lantern could cast and heard the fan for my central heat come on. Power had been restored.

Pinned between Mindy and the sofa, I was stiff from lying on my side all night. I wanted to move us to my bedroom but I chose to wait for it to warm up first. Ten minutes later, an urgent need to pee ended my wait. Mindy rolled onto her back when I extricated myself.

"I have to pee, too," she said when she heard me get up.

"Ladies first."

"Oh, you're such a gentleman, Freddie." Mindy looked

up at the ceiling light. "I see the power is back on. What should we do now?"

"The storm is probably passed over but it will take hours to clear the roads. For now, I suggest we spend the rest of the night in the master bedroom."

Mindy looked at my limp dick and smiled. "Fine with me. I have to do a children's Valentine Day event at YWCA tomorrow afternoon, what about you?"

"I'm scheduled to be off but will probably go in for a few hours to help out but that won't be until after we get your car on the road."

After we peed, we headed to bed.

* * *

The time was 6:05 AM and dawn was breaking. As I pulled back the sheets for Mindy, I whispered in her ear, "It's getting light outside. I'm going to call my assistant manager about opening the store. I'll be right back."

"Okay, baby."

On the way out, I grabbed Mindy's wet clothes from the bathroom and put them in the dryer. After sending a text to my assistant asking him to tell me when he was able to get to the store, I put my phone on the charger. I only had time to shutoff the fireplace before my phone buzzed.

The message from my assistant indicated he had just

arrived. I called him to discuss the situation and make recovery plans. He reported that roads were still icy but the skies were clear and the wind had died down. Another worker was already there and as we talked, a second arrived. Leaving the decision to him, I explained my need to help '*a friend*' before I stop by later in the day.

I climbed back into bed and Mindy rolled over to snuggle with a leg and arm draped over me. We shared a long, good morning kiss, followed by one of her hands fondling my cock. After getting hard once more, she asked, "Are we ready to get up yet?"

"I was out on the front porch about an hour ago and saw that the ice is starting to melt. You should call for Triple-A while I go shower. We should have time before we have to leave to get your car."

"Ok, Daddy," she said wrapping a towel around herself before dancing out of the bedroom to get her phone and make the call.

Mindy walked in wearing the silk robe right after I finished my shower. *Perhaps she waited to hear me shut*

off the water or the moment was just coincidental. Either way, she wasn't in the same mood as when she left.

"Bad news, the tow truck will be at my car in thirty minutes."

"Is that bad news?"

Mindy stared at my cock and whined, "We don't have time now even for a quickie, do we?"

"No, I'm afraid not."

She folded her arms and stood there pouting. To me, Mindy looked so sexy that way. She was staring continuously at my cock, her mouth opened and she stuck her tongue out. "I want it, Daddy!" She pouted.

I tried to end the titillating effect by blocking her sight of my cock with my towel. It wasn't working. I even tried sending her away. "Better get dressed, sweetie." As I spoke, my cock was straining upward.

Moments later, my cock was in a very warm and wet familiar place. I pulled the towel off my head to find her kneeling in front of me, her mouth vigorously sucking me off. I couldn't stop her; I didn't want to.

The second blowjob was very much like the first: incredibly exciting, a quick cumshot, and eagerly swallowed. I worried I might become a slave to Mindy's desires. If she demanded to fuck right then, I might have given in.

Mindy then stood up and explained, "I think a man

has a better day if he gets a blowjob to start things off. Now we gotta hurry to meet the tow truck."

"I do agree..." I chuckled.

* * *

We didn't even have time to drink the coffee I brewed. Mindy took my hand and led me into my bedroom where she had laid out her clothes taken from the dryer. Her clothes were nice and clean. I gave her one of Jill's wool coats to wear while I layered a jacket and sweater over my shirt and tie.

Traffic was light and we arrived at her car just as she received a text that the tow truck was nearby. Parking out of the way for the tow, we only had time to add each other's contact info on our cellphones.

When I saw the tow truck coming down the hill, I stepped out of my SUV to direct him to Mindy's car. I thought he would tow her car back to the road but discovered he anchored his truck at the pavement's edge and extended a cable down to her car. After I started her car and put it in neutral, the tow truck driver had me stand well out of the way as he began to winch her car toward his truck.

When Mindy's car was within a few feet of the tow truck, he hooked his boom to the undercarriage and towed the car onto the pavement. It only took fifteen minutes to complete the job. After Mindy signed an acknowledgement for the insurance company, the tow truck left for his next job.

Mindy had to go home to get ready for a Saturday Valentine's event and I was headed to the store, so we exchanged a long hug and several kisses. I promised to call her that evening, and then watched her drive away before getting in my car. On the short drive, I felt lonely and hoped a relationship with Mindy would fill the emptiness I had regarded as normal for years.

Chapter Nine

I got to the store quicker than I expected finding that all store operations were running smoothly. My assistant manager had already created a modified supply order for me to authorize. I visited all the departments, speaking with every employee and showing my appreciation for their hard work. I promised everyone who worked the day or the night before the storm would get free sandwiches for their families as well as a time-and-a-half bonus on their next paychecks.

When I was done talking about store operations, the memories of being with Mindy crowded my head. After the excitement of the night before, I wanted to spend many more nights including Valentine's Day making love to Mindy. I made up my mind to pursue it to the end with her regardless the gap between our ages.

While making my rounds, I saw our customers

buying wine, candy, and flowers for Valentine's Day. In past years, V-Day was just a regular event needing some particulars but not many preparations. This year, people were a bit more romantic and I noticed. The buying behaviors of our customers gave me exactly how I could show Mindy that she had won my heart.

* * *

I bought several bottles of the wine for the night before and a dozen roses. My cooking skills were nothing to rave about but I wanted to at least have a good meal for Mindy, hoping we would enjoy the night together again in the same steamy fashion. Our store has signature full-course-meals-in-a-box with simple instructions, so I chose a pot roast meal with mashed potatoes and broccoli. I threw in some chocolate-covered strawberries for dessert in my purchase.

The cashier that checked my items knew my past well, causing her to ask if I had a hot date. When I admitted that I did, she responded, "Good for you." Instead of finding excuses to hang around, I couldn't wait to leave.

* * *

When I got home, I shaved and showered again, then

dressed in my best casual clothes. Sitting down to call Mindy, I first rehearsed how to invite her because I was so out of the loop.

She answered on the second ring with a bubbly greeting, "Hi, Daddy'! I've been thinking of you all day. How was work?"

"Everything is fine. I could hardly concentrate today because I couldn't wait to see you again."

"I know what you mean. So you're home now?"

"Yes. Honey, I was calling to ask..."

Mindy cut me off with, "Hold those thoughts, Daddy. I have something really important to do. Can I call you back in about fifteen minutes?"

"Sure—sure, no problem."

* * *

I was a little disappointed because I was so anxious, but knew waiting would be worth the wait especially if we had wild sex again. I began to worry when thirty minutes passed and she didn't call. When the doorbell rang, I almost didn't answer because I didn't want to be bothered by a salesman or political canvasser.

When I opened the door, there stood Mindy wearing a red leather knee-length coat and matching high heels while holding a red balloon emblazoned with the words '*Be Mine*'. She yelled, "Happy Valentine's Day!" as she pulled her coat open to reveal she had on nothing but a lacy red teddy underneath. Her attire left me speechless until she said,"It's frigging cold out here. Aren't you going to let me in?"

Stepping aside, I said, "I'm sorry, but you look stunning like daddy's little girl. All I could think about was making love to you."

"Right there on your front porch? I didn't know you're into that kinky stuff, not that I'd mind if it was warm enough, but what would your neighbors say, Freddie?"

"My neighbors have never seen a woman visit me unless they saw us leaving this morning. Seeing us going at it in the day would be the neighborhood scandal. Are you really bold enough to fuck while somebody watches?"

"I certainly have exhibitionist tendencies. To be honest, I'd love to have somebody catch us fucking our brains out in your office at the store." I must have looked terrified because Mindy assured me that she would never really do something that will cause me to lose my job.

I pulled her close and kissed her. Her perfume gave me an instant erection. She felt it because she started rubbing her mound side-to-side across my bulge.

"I love making you hard because it means you want me as much as I want you. That's why I was so anxious to get back here. Well, that and wanting to ask you to be my

Valentine. By the way, what did you want to ask me on the phone?"

I put my arm around her waist and turned her to face the dining room table where I had settings for a exquisite romantic dinner. Besides the dishes, silverware, and napkins, she saw candles, wine, and a vase full of roses.

"Oh, Freddie! You are so sweet. What are we having?"

"Pot roast."

"Will it take long to make? Is it already done?"

"It takes forty-five minutes in the oven to heat up. I didn't start it yet because I didn't know if we'd see each other again tonight. You didn't let me ask you."

"Oh, Freddy! Don't be like that. You're acting like an old man."

I chuckled. "Yeah, you're right."

"Good."

"By the way, the wine you like and these roses are my way of asking you to be my Valentine. Everything worked out in the end but what would you have done if I wanted to take you out to dinner?"

Mindy giggled, "I've got that covered. I have an overnight bag in my trunk with clothes. I even have my work clothes for tomorrow in case I stay overnight. I hope you don't mind."

"Fucking-right. Next time bring all your clothes, young lady."

"Do you mean that?"

“Yes, I do. You should move in. I want you here every day because there's no denying it. I’m in love with you, Mindy."

She threw her arms around me, and peppered my cheek with kisses. "Oh, Freddie! I love you, too. I was so afraid we didn't have enough in common to overcome our age difference."

"Dinner will be ready shortly. Until then...“ I said as I scooped Mindy up into my arms and carried her to the bedroom.

The End

www.ingramcontent.com/pod-product-compliance
Lightning Source LLC
Chambersburg PA
CBHW070427170726
48291CB00002B/395